Geronimo Stilton

THE AMAZING VOYAGE

THE THIRD ADVENTURE IN THE KINGDOM OF FANTASY

Scholastic Inc.
New York   Toronto   London   Auckland
Sydney   Mexico City   New Delhi   Hong Kong

No part of this publication may be reproduced, stored in a retrieval system, or transmitted in any form or by any means, electronic, mechanical, photocopying, recording, or otherwise, without written permission from the copyright holder. For information regarding permission, please contact: Atlantyca S.p.A., Via Leopardi 8, 20123 Milan, Italy; e-mail foreignrights@atlantyca.it, www.atlantyca.com.

ISBN 978-0-545-30771-0

Copyright © 2007 by Edizioni Piemme S.p.A., Via Tiziano 32, 20145 Milan, Italy.

International Rights © Atlantyca S.p.A.

English translation © 2011 by Atlantyca S.p.A.

GERONIMO STILTON names, characters, and related indicia are copyright, trademark, and exclusive license of Atlantyca S.p.A. All rights reserved. The moral right of the author has been asserted.

Based on an original idea by Elisabetta Dami.

www.geronimostilton.com

Published by Scholastic Inc., 557 Broadway, New York, NY 10012. SCHOLASTIC and associated logos are trademarks and/or registered trademarks of Scholastic Inc.

Stilton is the name of a famous English cheese. It is a registered trademark of the Stilton Cheese Makers' Association. For more information, go to www.stiltoncheese.com

Text by Geronimo Stilton
Original title *Terzo viaggio nel regno della fantasia*
Cover by Giuseppe Ferrario
Illustrations by Danilo Barozzi, Silvia Bigolin, Giuseppe Di Dio, Giuseppe Guindani, Barbara Pellizzari, Umberto Pezzoli, and the Piemme archives
Color by Christian Aliprandi

Special thanks to Kathryn Cristaldi
Translated by Julia Heim
Interior design by Kay Petronio

12 11 10 9 8 7 6 5 4 3   11 12 13 14 15 16/0

Printed in Singapore   46
First printing, September 2011

Geronimo Stilton

I am the publisher of *The Rodent's Gazette,* the most famouse newspaper on Mouse Island. This is my third trip to the **KINGDOM OF FANTASY**.

Strongheart the Giant

I live in a beautiful mansion, and my best friend is a falcon. My dream is to meet my true love.

King Thunderhorn

I am the King of the Elves. I have snowy white fur, and my horns and hooves are made of gold.

Sterling

I am the Princess of the Silver Dragons. I am not afraid to go into battle, and I know all the tricks to tame a dragon!

Puss in Boots

I am the Ambassador of the Land of Fairy Tales. I like to act tough, but I'm really a softy deep down. (Shhh! Don't tell anyone!)

Horizon

I'm a blue boat built of magic wood from the Talking Forest. I can speak and sail all by myself.

Beatrice Bigfoot

I am a giant from the Land of the Southern Giants. I get captured by the trolls in this story. But don't worry . . . there's a happy ending.

SPRING
HAS SPRUNG!

It all started just like this . . .

It was a beautiful, sunny spring day. Well, to be exact, it was the very first day of **spring**. The sky in New Mouse City was crystal clear, and the smell of flowers filled the air. I sniffed the air and smiled. Spring had officially SPRUNG!

Don't you just love spring? I do! I listened to the birds CHIRPING outside my window. Sunshine warmed my back, and the smell of cherry blossoms filled my office. I tried to do some work but . . .

I love spring!

1

Oh, how rude! I forgot to introduce myself. My name is Geronimo Stilton. I run *The Rodent's Gazette*, the most famouse newspaper on Mouse Island.

Anyway, where was I? Oh, yes — I was having a little trouble concentrating, due to the **sun**, and the ƒℓowers, and the birds, and . . . Well, you get the idea.

Right then the door to my office burst open.

"Uncle!" a little mouse shrieked with delight. It was my dear nephew Benjamin. He gave me a **hug**.

" Can I have dinner at your house tonight?"

he asked.

"Great idea," I replied with a **smile**. "How about we have a **PIZZA** party with the

whole family? We can **CELEBRATE** the first day of SPRING."

Here is the editorial office of The Rodent's Gazette.

The
Rodent's
Gazette

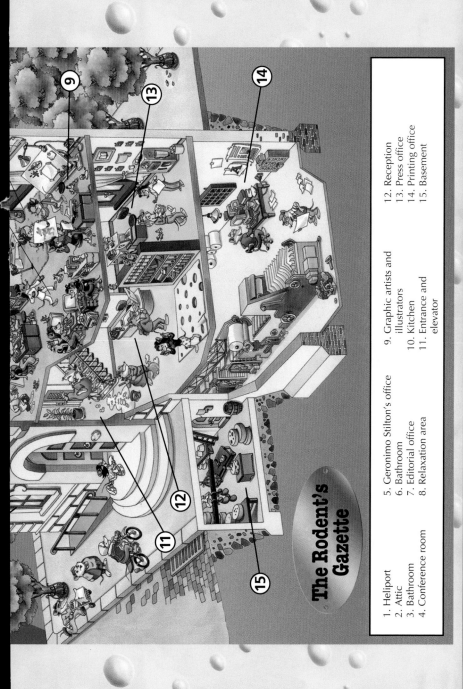

The Rodent's Gazette

1. Heliport
2. Attic
3. Bathroom
4. Conference room
5. Geronimo Stilton's office
6. Bathroom
7. Editorial office
8. Relaxation area
9. Graphic artists and illustrators
10. Kitchen
11. Entrance and elevator
12. Reception
13. Press office
14. Printing office
15. Basement

GERONIMO STILTON'S HOUSE

CHOMP! CHOMP! CHOMP!

That night the Stilton family gathered at my house. My sister, Thea, was there, my cousin Trap, Grandfather Shortpaws, Aunt Sweetfur . . .

Even Petunia Pretty Paws came with her brother, **WOLFGANG**. Too bad Petunia also brought along her pesky niece, Bugsy Wugsy. I made sure Bugsy sat **far** away from me.

My cousin Trap made all kinds of **pizzas**: some with just **TOMATO SAUCE**, some with **PEPPERONI**, some with **mushrooms**, some with different types of **cheese**, and even some with **HAM** and pineapple.

I ate so many slices I lost count!

CHOMP! CHOMP! CHOMP!

My belly got rounder and rounder, but I couldn't stop. The pizza was so **DELICIOUS**!

Finally, everyone finished eating and left. I ate one more slice. Then I waddled off to bed.

I Tossed and I Turned

That night I tossed and I turned, and I tossed and I turned in bed. . . .

I felt like I had swallowed a **bowling ball**. Oh, why had I gobbled up all that pizza?

Since I couldn't sleep, I decided to try reading. After all, there's nothing like a good **BOOK** to take my mind off my problems.

But without thinking, I picked up a book about ghosts and haunted houses. It was so **SCARY**!

Now, instead of getting sleepy, I was even more awake.

(1) At midnight on the dot, I got up to make myself my thirty-first cup of chamomile tea. (I had already had thirty cups before that.)

(2) But my paws got all twisted up in the sheets! I tripped, and the pile of thirty cups that I had placed on the nightstand **crashed** to the ground.

3 They **SMASHED** into a thousand pieces.

4 As I tried to keep my balance, I cut my paw on a **SHARP** shard.

5 I **RAN** to the bathroom to look for a **BANDAGE**, but I slipped on a puddle of water.

6 Then I **hit** my head on the edge of the sink!

As I was fainting, I remembered that there was water on the floor because the toilet was leaking. I had forgotten to call the **plumber**!

Geronimo's toilet

"Oops, the p...

4

Ouch ouch ouch!

I hurt my paw on a sharp shard.

I ran to the bathroom to look for a bandage, but I slipped on a puddle of water.

5

Oops!

6

Bang!

I hit my head on the edge of the sink and fainted!

I COULDN'T SEE
A THING!

When I came to, I felt something wet licking my face. I gulped. Was it a **GHOST** with a taste for mice?

The room was pitch-black. 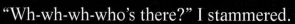 **I COULDN'T SEE A THING!** Then I realized I still had my eyes closed. When I opened them, the room was still dark, except for two enormous **GOLDEN EYES** peering down at me.

"Wh-wh-wh-who's there?" I stammered.

A voice sang out:

"Don't be afraid, you already know me. I come to you from the Kingdom of Fantasy!"

I gasped. Now I knew who it was. It was my old friend the *Dragon of the Rainbow*!

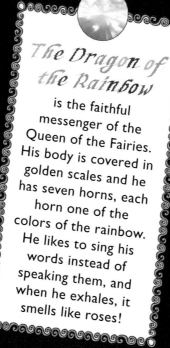

The Dragon of the Rainbow

is the faithful messenger of the Queen of the Fairies. His body is covered in golden scales and he has seven horns, each horn one of the colors of the rainbow. He likes to sing his words instead of speaking them, and when he exhales, it smells like roses!

I turned on the **light** and grinned. I knew the dragon well from my adventures in the Kingdom of Fantasy.

Then I heard another familiar voice. Well, actually it was more of a croak.

"**SIR KNIGHT!**" the voice called.

A frog in a **red** jacket clung to the back of the dragon. It was Scribblehopper. We had met on my first trip to the Kingdom of Fantasy. He **STILL** thought I was a knight no matter how much I tried to correct him!

But why had he come looking for me?

KIDNAPPED!

I found out soon enough. It seemed **Blossom**, *the Queen of the Fairies*, had been kidnapped! "The **QUEEN OF THE WITCHES** kidnapped her!" Scribblehopper wailed. Then he handed me a scroll.

TRY TO DECIPHER THE MESSAGE!*

* You will find the Fantasian Alphabet on page 291.

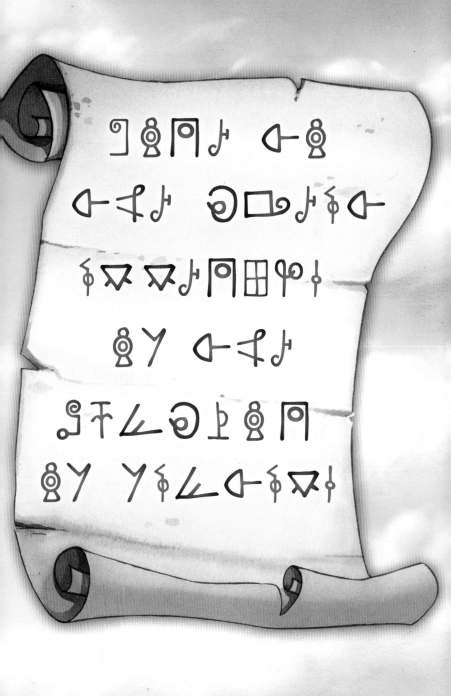

The scroll was written in the Fantasian Alphabet. Lucky for me, I had learned the Fantasian Alphabet on one of my adventures to the kingdom.

"The gnomes are holding a **big** meeting and they need your help," Scribblehopper explained. "So come on, Sir Knight. Lose the pajamas and shake a paw! The **Kingdom of Fantasy** is in great danger!"

As I got dressed, Scribblehopper read me a few bad poems he had written, sang three songs he had composed, and chatted **on** and **on** and **on** and **on**.

Cheese niblets! I had forgotten how much that frog could croak!

"Okay, okay!" I finally squeaked. "I'm ready to go. Just please stop **croaking** for a minute. I can't hear myself **THiNK!**"

Scribblehopper grinned. "No problemo, Sir Knight," he said. "But you know you can't really **HEAR** yourself think, because . . ."

He chatted on and on as the *Dragon of the Rainbow* rose into the sky.

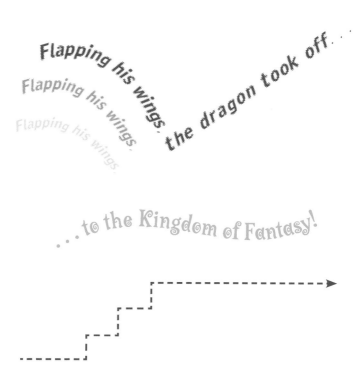

Flapping his wings.

Flapping his wings.

Flapping his wings.

Flapping his wings, the dragon took off . . .

. . . to the Kingdom of Fantasy!

I clung nervously to one of the dragon's many scales. Every time I take a trip to the Kingdom of Fantasy, I mean to talk to him about adding some **seat belts** for safety purposes, but I always forget!

Still, as we soared into the **fluffy** clouds, I began to relax.

The night sky was *beautiful*. The air was fresh, and the moon was as **round** as a perfect slice of provolone.

The Voyage to the
Kingdom of Fantasy!

To the Kingdom

The trip took all night. At dawn
we flew over the Kingdom of
the Fairies. I waited for the air
to fill with the smell of spring
flowers. But when I looked
down, I saw that the land was
covered in snow!

A SAD AND
FREEZING WINTER

"Why is there so much snow?" I asked Scribblehopper. "And where is the CRYSTAL CASTLE?"

The frog let out a low sigh. "Alas, it's been a sad and **freezing** winter, Your Knightliness. Except for the steeple, the whole castle is buried in **SNOW**!"

He pointed to the huge stretch of ice beneath us. The only thing sticking out was a steeple with a SILVER STAR on it. I couldn't believe it. It was the star that shone from the very top of Blossom's castle.

Scribblehopper sniffed once. Then twice. Then he began to BAWL like a tadpole. "Boo-hoo-hoo!" It was so cold his tears turned to ice and fell to the ground with a terrible plink, plink, plink!

Cheese niblets! I was getting a mouse-sized headache.

I didn't know what was worse: listening to Scribblehopper's LOUD ICICLE TEARS or listening to one of his terrible poems!

Snow

a poem by Scribblehopper,
Literary Frog

WHAT DOES A FROG KNOW ABOUT SNOW?
IT'S COLD AND IT'S WET
AND IT FREEZES MY TOES.
IT COVERS THE PONDS
AND THE STREAMS AND THE LAKES.
IT PUTS OUT THE FLAMES
ON MY FLY BIRTHDAY CAKES.
OH, ONCE I WAS HAPPY
IN WARM, SUNNY AIR,
FLOATING ON LILY PADS
WITHOUT A CARE.

BUT A WITCH CAME ALONG
AND SENT SNOW FALLING DOWN,
SO NOW THIS POOR FROG
WEARS A PERMANENT FROWN!

Yours Froggerly,
Scribblehopper

A Huge Smoke Cloud

We hurried toward the Kingdom of the Gnomes to make it in time for the **Great Assembly**.

As we got closer, the sky became **GRAYER** and **GRAYER**.

Then I noticed a huge **smoke cloud** coming from the west. It was bringing with it a freezing wind as **cold** as a witch's breath!

The smoke was preventing the **sun's rays** from reaching the ground, which was why it was so cold!

There was so much smoke!

I KNEW YOU'D MAKE IT!

COZY **FACTUAL**

Finally, we landed in the Kingdom of the Gnomes. I found Cozy and Factual, the Queen and King of the Gnomes, in the **throne room**. The king ran to greet me.

"Oh, thank goodness you're here, Knight! We're all so worried about Blossom. Tomorrow the Great Assembly will meet. All of the heroes of the *kingdom* will be here."

The queen grabbed my paw.

"I knew you'd make it, brave knight."

I gulped. Me? **BRAVE?**

The queen pumped her little fist in the air.

"Good will triumph!" she cried.

The words rang in the air. . . .

Good will triumph!
Good will triumph!
Good will triumph!
Good will triumph!
Good will triumph!
Good will triumph!
Good will triumph!
Good will triumph!
Good will triumph!

PROBLEM?
WHAT PROBLEM?

The queen turned to me and smiled.

"Dear Knight, you must be TIRED," she said. "We will prepare the guest room for you."

But just then a little gnome began whispering furiously in the queen's ear.

"Problem? What problem?" the queen asked IMPATIENTLY.

The gnome blushed. "He — I mean, the knight — that one there, I mean . . . he won't fit! He's too big!"

The queen laughed kindly.

"Take him to the ballroom, the room with the highest ceilings in the palace," she said. "The ROYAL CARPENTERS can put together ten of the beds. The ROYAL TAILORS can sew some pajamas and a warm blanket from ten of the curtains. And the royal cooks can prepare a meal fit to feed fifty gnomes."

I thanked the queen for her generosity. She really was the sweetest gnome I knew. Not that I knew many gnomes back home!

Later the queen told me a happy bedtime story as a chorus of gnomes sang me a gentle lullaby.

There's no place like Gnome. There's no place like Gnome,

I thought as I drifted off to sleep.

THE ROYAL CARPENTERS . . .
constructed a bed for me made out of **TEN** of their little beds!

THE ROYAL TAILORS . . .
sewed some pajamas and a beautiful multicolored blanket for me from ten curtains!

THE ROYAL COOKS . . .
prepared so, so, so much food for me, because I was so, so, so hungry!

THE LATEST GNOME STYLE!

The next morning, the queen surprised me.

"I know you have an INVISIBLE suit of armor, Knight," she said. "But you need something warmer. So I asked all the GNOMES in the land to sew you these clothes made of the *warmest wool*. They're the latest in gnome style!"

I created the pattern.

I gave the advice.

I laid it out to dry.

I fastened it.

I stuffed it.

I sewed it.

I brought the bandages.

I chose the fabric.

I washed the fabric.

I ironed it.

I cut it.

I threaded the needles.

I pricked my fingers.

On the TAG they had sewn my name:

GERONIMO
STILTON

I was touched. It must have taken the gnomes all night to make such *beautiful* clothes!

"Thank you," I said. The gnomes waited outside while I tried the clothes on. Then I called them back and took a deep bow. The clothes fit **PERFECTLY**!

Thank you, kind ladies!

I sewed a sleeve.

I made the buttonholes.

I stitched the pants.

I stitched the hat.

I shined the boots.

I did the other sleeve.

I attached the buttons.

I made the hem.

I sewed the socks.

Oh, how elegant the knight looks!

THE GREAT ASSEMBLY

Just then I looked out from the balcony and saw a dust cloud on the horizon. The friends of Queen Blossom and the Kingdom of the Fairies were arriving!

"**Here they come!**" cried the gnomes. I leaned over the balcony to get a better look.

What an **incredible** sight!

There were pixies dressed in green flying on the TRANSPARENT wings of dragonflies. DRAGONS let out threatening FLAMES from their mouths as a band of UNICORNS galloped nearby.

I even recognized Boils the chameleon, Goose

Blahblah, and Oscar Roach from my previous trip to the **Kingdom of Fantasy**.

There were tons of **elves** with silver bows.

silver bow

And I spotted Puss in Boots from the Land of Fairy Tales.

Sea creatures approached from the water. Their queen was traveling in a **CRYSTAL** tub. I guess she didn't want to get her fish tail wet.

fish tail

Farther away in the river I noticed a **shimmering** blue boat with luminous silk sails. The boat was beautiful. I wondered what land it came from.

Blossom's Friends and Allies

ELVES are noble, generous, and loyal. They know the woods and can run swiftly and silently.

SILVER DRAGONS are strong and courageous. They love justice and goodness.

Pixies are small and dress in green. They are able to navigate the forests.

Unicorns live in the Valley of the Blue Unicorns.

Sea Creatures include mermaids, dolphins, and whales.

Strongheart the Giant and Puss in Boots walked all the way from the Land of the Northern Giants and the Land of Fairy Tales.

NO PUSHING!
NO SHOVING!

Together everyone gathered on the great lawn in front of the palace. I looked around wide-eyed. Blossom had so many friends, the place was **JAM-PACKED**!

Unicorns stood shoulder to shoulder with fire-breathing dragons. Elves and pixies claimed seats on the **snow-covered** trees.

"Please, no pushing! No shoving!" Queen Cozy called.

Then King Factual held up his hand for ꜱɪʟᴇɴᴄᴇ.

"I guess there's no good way to say this, so I'll just say it," he began. "**QUEEN BLOSSOM IS IN DANGER!**" he announced. "She has been kidnapped by the Queen of the Witches!"

The crowd went wild.

"No!" I heard someone cry.

"Not *sweet* Blossom!" another sobbed.

But King Factual held up his hand again. "Well, don't just sit there crying about it," he said, jumping to his feet. "Let's go save her!"

I let out a tiny cough.

"Um, Your Majesty, n-no offense," I stammered, "but you're missing one small detail."

"Detail? What detail?" he muttered. "I'm very good with details. . . ."

I hated to insult the king's *intelligence*, but what could I do?

"We can't run off to save the queen because we don't know where she is," I explained.

A **hush** fell over the crowd.

Then an elf shouted out, "Uh, if you don't know where she is, how are we supposed to save her?"

"**YEAH!**" all the dragons chorused.

King Factual scratched his head, looking perplexed. **UH-OH**, I thought. Would the crowd get **angry**? Would they **storm the palace**?

Headlines flashed in my brain: *Angry Mob Wrecks Gnome Home! Gnome Meeting Ends in Madness!*

"I've got an idea!" Boils shouted out. "Years ago, Blossom gave the gnomes a **silver** case. She said to open it if the Kingdom of Fantasy was ever in grave *danger*!"

The king lit up. "That's right! It's in the **LIBRARY**!"

I tried to thank Boils for his good idea, but I couldn't see him.

He had blended in to the surroundings, as usual.

CAN YOU SEE WHERE
BOILS IS HIDING?

I POINT TO BLOSSOM

I headed to the library with Boils and the king and queen. The case was made of **precious** silver, formed into the shape of a *rose*.

It was delicately crafted, and it **shined** like thousands and thousands of **lights**. Around each of the petals were hundreds of **pure diamonds**.

The King of the Gnomes put a *tiny* key into the lock.

We all held our breath.

Inside was a silver compass encased in **diamonds**. There was writing in the Fantasian Alphabet on it. ......

Inside the case there was also a scroll with another message. ......

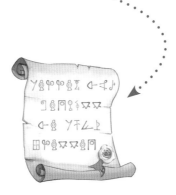

Turn the page to try to decode the message!

Inside, there were a silver compass encased in diamonds . . .

TRY TO DECODE THE MESSAGE!*

*You can find the Fantasian Alphabet on page 291.

. . . and a scroll!

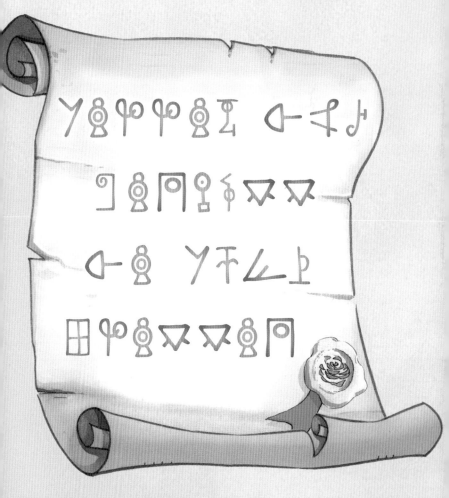

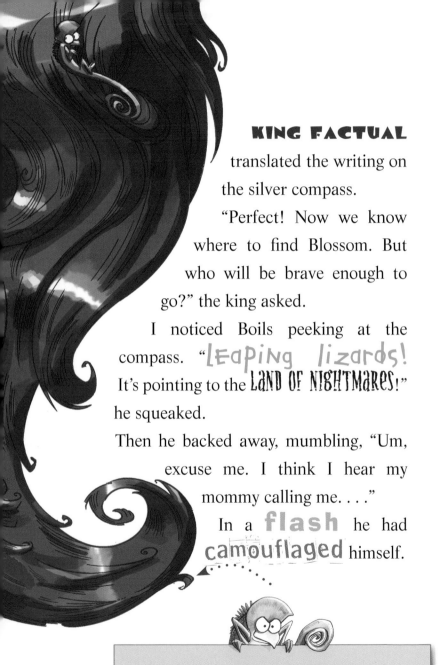

KING FACTUAL
translated the writing on the silver compass.

"Perfect! Now we know where to find Blossom. But who will be brave enough to go?" the king asked.

I noticed Boils peeking at the compass. "Leaping lizards! It's pointing to the LAND OF NIGHTMARES!" he squeaked.

Then he backed away, mumbling, "Um, excuse me. I think I hear my mommy calling me. . . ."

In a flash he had camouflaged himself.

CAN YOU FIND BOILS?

THE FANTASY COMPANY!

Once outside again the king addressed the crowd. "Who will save Blossom? Who will join **the FaNtaSy CompaNy**?"

I looked around. No one was listening. The elves were playing patty-cake, the dragons were *chasing* their tails, and the sea creatures were *twirling* on the **frozen** river. How rude!

I felt so bad for the king that before I knew what I was doing, I stepped forward.

"Ahem, I, Stilton of Geronimo — I mean, Geronimo of Stilton — I mean, *Geronimo Stilton*, will join," I stammered.

Queen Cozy hugged me. "Dear Knight, you are so **brave**. Here, take this vial of **dragon tears**. It can cure any wound."

DRAGON TEAR

THUMP! THUMP!! THUMP!!!

A minute later I felt the ground **shake**.

THUMP! THUMP!! THUMP!!!

From behind the hills, a creature the size of a fifteen-story building appeared.

It was Strongheart, my friend the giant!

I jumped back so that he wouldn't squash me like one of Great-Aunt Ratsy's sweet potato and cream cheese pancakes.

Strongheart can be a little distracted at times.

When he spotted me, he picked me up in his giant hand and held me at eye level.

"It's good to see you, friend," he said.

I tried to speak but I was suddenly having trouble breathing. The giant's breath was so bad

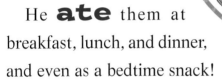

it could have knocked out a whole army of mice! It was then that I remembered how much the giant loved **onions**.

He **ate** them at breakfast, lunch, and dinner, and even as a bedtime snack!

He ate them stuffed, **fried**, **baked**, **PICKLED**, and even **raw**!

"How are you, Sir Knight?" he thundered.

Even though his breath was killing me, I didn't want to be rude. So I choked out, "GOOD, and you?"

The giant sighed, nearly knocking me flat on my back with his breath. "Well, I am happy I've made lots of friends, but I am still looking for my **one true love**. You know, that special someone," he murmured.

THE GIANT'S
STINKY SANDWICH

Here is the giant's snack!

The giant stared off into space. "Someday I'd like to have a family with a *wife* and some *little giants*. Well, they won't be *little* if they're **giants**, but you know what I mean," he continued *dreamily*.

Suddenly, the giant blinked.

"Oops, I forgot where I was for a moment," he said. Then he announced,

"I WILL JOIN THE COMPANY!"
The crowd **CHEERED**.

STRONGHEART
The last of the giants

STRONGHEART

STRONGHEART

of the Great Falcon,
the last of the Northern giants

e is part of the noble Great Falcon clan and a friend to Geronimo. On Geronimo's first visit to the Kingdom of Fantasy, Geronimo helped the giant rediscover his name: Strongheart!

His story is a sad one: His entire family was consumed by the White Fury, a terrible avalanche that covered Falcon's Beak, the giants' palace, many years ago.

Strongheart is the only survivor of all the sons of the last King of the Giants, and therefore he is heir to the throne.

In his saddlebag he always keeps the crowns of the King and Queen of the Giants, because there is no one left in his kingdom.

He also keeps a bunch of extra onions in his bag, and eats them constantly, even for breakfast. This is why his breath always stinks!

He is often very lonely and wishes someday to have a family to fill his enormous castle with laughter and love.

THUNDERHORN, KING OF THE ELVES

The crowd was still cheering when a deep voice called out, "I am not afraid to go to the LaND OF NIGHTMaReS! I, too, will help save our dear Queen Blossom!"

Everyone turned around to see who was speaking. An EXTRAORDINARY creature strode across the great lawn. I cleaned my glasses to make sure I was seeing clearly. Yes, I was. The creature was a **deer**. An absolutely breathtaking, magnificent white deer!

He had a powerful, robust body and strong, muscular legs. He had shiny hooves and glittering golden horns. A **golden** pendant with an **oak**

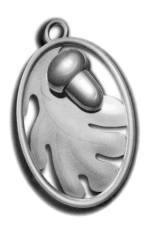

leaf hung around his neck.

I wondered what the oak leaf meant. Then Scribblehopper whispered, "See that oak leaf, Your Knightliness? That's the symbol of the Kingdom of the Elves. He must be some kind of elf messenger."

The deer fixed his **DARK EYES** on the crowd. "I am Thunderhorn, King of the Elves!" he exclaimed.

"I WILL JOIN THE COMPANY!"

I smiled at Thunderhorn. We needed all the help we could get to save Blossom.

Thurnderhorn,
King of the Elves

Oak Tree from the Kingdom of the Elves

THUNDERHORN

Thunderhorn

The mysterious King of the Elves

The elves are a noble and ancient people who love the forest and freedom.

The mysterious King of the Elves is never seen by foreigners in his true form — he always appears as a majestic white deer with gold horns and hooves.

He loves tranquility and the silence of his woods. Around his neck he wears a precious golden pendant with an oak leaf, the symbol of strength and wisdom, on it. He is always ready to defend those in difficulty and to listen to those who are in need of advice.

His name is Thunderhorn, and he is also called by these names: He Who Guards His People, the Bearer of Peace, the Keeper of Elf Wisdom, and the Protector of the Elf Woods.

His palace is the Golden Castle. It is surrounded by a deep forest, which is impenetrable to most: Only those with pure and noble souls can cross through it.

Sterling, Princess of the Silver Dragons

A slender young girl with BLOND BRAIDED hair stepped forward next.

She looked neither old nor young. She was very pretty, with wide GREEN eyes and a perfect oval face. Her delicate nose pointed upward, her lips were as *red* as cherries, and her skin was white and DeLiCATe, like porcelain. All the clothes she was wearing were made of different silver fabrics. She had a long silver coat and a SHINY silver vest of armor.

A silver bow and a quiver filled with **ARROWS** hung around her neck.

"My name is Sterling," she

announced, facing the crowd.

"I am the Princess of the SILVER Dragons." She pulled a silver flute out of her bag. When she blew into the flute, a flock of dragons appeared in the sky. Their shiny silver scales GLEAMED.

One of the dragons trotted over to Sterling.

"This is Sparkle," she said. "She will come with me on this mission."

Sterling took an ornate book out of her bag. It had precious silver designs on it and smelled like delicate lavender.

"I will bring this book, too. It is a magic book all about dragons. It can teach one everything there is to know about training a dragon," she said.

"I WILL JOIN THE COMPANY!"

Again the crowd clapped and cheered.

I smiled at Sterling, but her expression remained serious. This princess was all **business**.

Sterling, Princess
of the Silver Dragons

THE MAGIC BOOK
OF DRAGONS

This is Sterling's book. Secrets inside!

STERLING

STERLING
Princess of the Silver Dragons

In the fabulous Kingdom of the Silver Dragons lives a princess named Sterling. She is as beautiful as she is courageous and proud. Her titles are Princess of the Silver Dragons, Leader of Light, Keeper of the Secrets of the Flame, and Guardian of the Dragon Kingdom.

She is a wonderful archer and an expert swordswoman, but her bow and arrow are special because they won't hurt you. Instead, they will heal you! Her weapons are made of light, and they are capable of transforming those who are hit by turning their evil thoughts into good thoughts.

Sterling is a Silver Dragon tamer. To train them she uses a silver flute and a magic book, which contains all the secrets of her people. Sterling trains her Silver Dragons to fly in the most difficult conditions and to do acrobatics.

In her land there is even a training field just for dragons! There is a landing platform and a lake where dragons like to go to cool down their flaming throats.

PUSS IN BOOTS

Next a creature with bushy gray **FUR** stepped forward. **Holey cheese**! It was a giant **CAT**! His golden eyes seemed to bore right into mine.

He was dressed in **RED** boots and a large brimmed hat. At his side hung a sword with an **EMERALD-STUDDED** handle. But it wasn't his sword that was making me *nervous* — it was his **CLAWS**. They were as sharp as daggers!

I gulped.

"So **purrrrfectly** pleased to join you," he meowed, never taking his eyes off me. "My name is **GRAY**, but everyone knows me as Puss in Boots, or the Talking Cat, or the Not-So-Itty-Bitty Kitty, or Murderer of Mice, or, as my grandma Furball calls me, Mr. Tinkles — but don't repeat that one or I'll have to **eat you**!"

Then he roared with laughter.

I was so scared I thought I would die of FRIGHT.

"Ahem, well, um, yes, well, um, very nice to meet you," I managed to squeak.

GRAY opened his eyes wide. Then he licked his lips.

"You sure are a **BIG** mouse," he murmured. "But I was just pulling your paw. Of course I wouldn't eat you. After all, you *are* a friend of Blossom's, right? We're all on the same team."

Then he bent down and whispered in my ear, "Actually, I prefer fish, but I don't want to look

like a wimp in front of the crowd. You understand, don't you, Knightsy?"

I tried not to **gag**. Gray wasn't kidding about the fish. His breath reeked!

"I WILL JOIN THE COMPANY!"

GRAY,
PUSS IN BOOTS

SWEET-AND-SOUR
FISH FRY

PUSS IN BOOTS
Ambassador to the Land of Fairy Tales

 is real name is Gray, but he is also called Puss in Boots, the Talking Cat, the Not-So-Itty-Bitty Kitty, Murderer of Mice, and Mr. Tinkles.

He is the Ambassador of the Land of Fairy Tales, where all the characters from the fairy tales and legends of the world live.

He knows every language of the Kingdom of Fantasy and of the real world, because fairy tales are told everywhere on earth!

He loves playing pranks and tormenting his friends with tricks. He also loves dressing in expensive clothes and has so many pairs of boots he built ten floor-to-ceiling shoe racks to hold them.

He will eat mice if he is hungry, but he prefers the taste of fish.

PUSS IN BOOTS

HORIZON, THE TALKING SHIP

Right then, I heard a voice calling from the river,

"**YOO-HOO!** Over here! I would also like to join the company!"

I looked around but I didn't see anyone.

The voice laughed. "I'm right here, Sir Knight. I'm a talking ship. My name is HORIZON," she said.

HORIZON

And then I saw her. In the river next to the Gnome Palace floated a beautiful blue WOODEN ship with SILVER sails.

The ship didn't have a mouth, but when she spoke, the whole thing vibrated like a musical instrument.

"I am the Ambassador of the TALKING FOREST. I am built from MAGIC wood, which is why I can speak," Horizon explained.

A talking ship? I was impressed.

I couldn't shake the ship's paw, so I climbed aboard and patted her wheel.

"WELCOME TO THE COMPANY!"

the crowd cheered.

HORIZON, THE TALKING SHIP

MORE ALIVE
THAN DEAD?

At last, it seemed the Fantasy Company was complete.

That evening, in front of the Great Assembly of the Kingdom of Fantasy, there was a ceremony. We all put our right hands over our hearts and declared a solemn oath.

WE SWEAR:
TO ALWAYS GET ALONG!
TO STAND UP FOR THE POOR,
THE WEAK, AND THE DEFENSELESS!
TO LISTEN TO OTHERS!
TO NEVER LITTER!
TO RECYCLE WHENEVER POSSIBLE!
AND TO WASH UP AFTER
EVERY MEAL!

Then the King of the Gnomes stood up and declared:

> **"GOOD LUCK FINDING BLOSSOM! AND MAY YOU ALL COME BACK MORE ALIVE THAN DEAD!"**

I chewed my whiskers. More **ALIVE** than **DEAD**? What was that supposed to mean?!

After the ceremony, we all went to bed, but I was so **nervous** I couldn't sleep a wink.

At dawn, we prepared to leave. I was so tired I felt like a **ZOMBIE**. I said good-bye to all my friends.

Scribblehopper gave me a scroll with a poem he had written in my honor.

"If you don't make it back alive, I promise I'll make you a beautiful tombstone," he told me.

GERONIMO STILTON

The Fantasy
Company's
Departure!

Don't Burn Your Paws!

The King and Queen of the Gnomes said good-bye next.

Queen Cozy gave me a **warm bundle** of something that smelled delicious.

"Dear Knight, I've packed you some of my special **honey-glazed** sugar cookies. They're still **HOT** from the oven, so don't burn your paws," she warned.

My stomach rumbled in response, and she laughed. I was tempted to forget the whole trip and just spend the day eating **cookies**.

But instead, I looked around for Boils so I could say good-bye.

As usual, he had **CAMOUFLAGED** himself!

TURN THE PAGE TO SEE WHERE BOILS IS HIDING!

SWEET TREATS FROM
Queen Cozy

HONEY-GLAZED
SUGAR COOKIES

Excuse Me, Mr. Tinkles!

At last we were ready to climb aboard the talking ship. Even though I was extremely nervous about the journey, I was **excited**, too. I mean, who gets a chance to sail on a ship that **TALKS**?!

But when we got on deck, Gray muttered, "Where are the sailors? How are we supposed to move this thing?"

"Excuse me, Mr. Tinkles!" Horizon fumed. "I told you I'm magical. I know how to sail by myself."

"Hey, don't call me Mr. tinkles!" Gray yelled.

Then the **giant** shouted, "Quit arguing, you two. LIFT your anchor, lady, and let's go!"

I twisted my tail in a knot. So much for getting along.

I knelt down and said, "Please lift your anchor, Horizon. Think of Queen Blossom."

Eventually, Horizon lifted her anchor and off we went.

"What a sensitive ship," Gray mumbled.

A minute later he was soaking wet. "Watch it, cat, or I'll throw you overboard!" Horizon yelled.

Soon we were skimming through the blue waves, sending up splashes of foam. It was amazing to watch as the **HELM** of the ship steered itself.

Later, when Horizon grew tired, dolphins, whales, and giant sea creatures helped move her along.

During the trip, I spoke to the ship about all the wonderful places she had

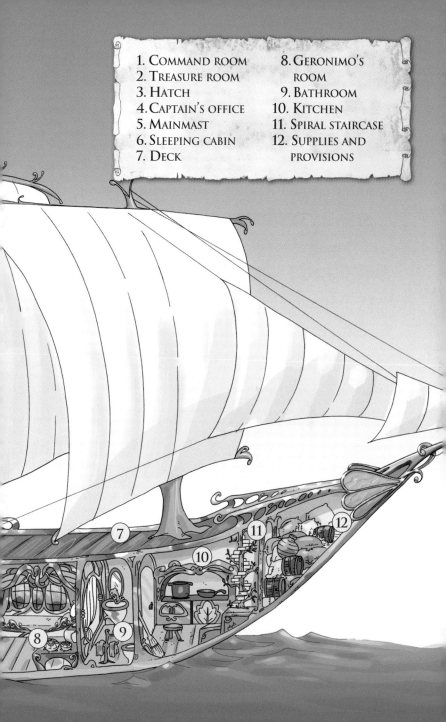

visited and the adventures she had been through. I found out Horizon was one FASCINATING ship!

The ship had lots of rooms, including one that was just for **treasure**! Every room GLEAMED with touches of silver — a mirror, a painting, a SPARKLING sink. The place was beautiful.

One evening I went on deck to thank Horizon for letting us sail with her.

She thanked me, too. "You're the only passenger who doesn't make a **mess**," she

explained. "The **CAT** leaves *fur* everywhere and the **giant** runs up and down, making me unbalanced. **STERLING** clipped one of my sails with an arrow. And the deer ꮪꮯꭱꮧꭲꮯꞕꮛꮪ the deck with his hooves!"

I shook my head. Talk about letting people walk all over you!

Then Horizon said, "You are such a kind knight, Geronimo of Stilton. I would like to give you a gift. Go to the **treasure room** and open the **SILVER** chest."

Cheese niblets! The treasure room! I was so excited.

I ran to the room and **FLUNG** open the chest. Inside was a SHINY silver suit of elf armor. There was also a ring. It seemed like it was made of LIGHT.

THE RING OF LIGHT

"I know you are a **fearless knight**," Horizon said. "But even you will need help in freeing Blossom. This *Ring of Light* will help you. The ring will emit a sword of white light made of pure energy."

I put on the ring. It was encased in pure CRYSTAL. I noticed that inside the ring there was writing in Fantasian.

Can you translate it?

TRY TO DECIPHER WHAT IS WRITTEN!*

*You will find the Fantasian Alphabet on page 291.

Gigantic yellow gold

The giants melted their jewels to obtain the metal for the Rings of Light.

Magic crystal

The stones are pure crystal and come from the Cavern of the Fairies.

Fantasian writing

The engraving on the Rings of Light reads "Only for peace."

RINGS OF LIGHT

In the Kingdom of Fantasy, there are some very precious rings known as the Rings of Light.

They were made during the Time of Night, in the heart of the Crystal Cave of the Fairies, as a symbol of peace, harmony, and unity among the people.

🔹 🔹 🔹

Every kingdom participated in the creation of the rings. The giants melted the precious metal; the dragons used their fire to heat them; the elves worked on them; the gnomes, with their small but able hands, made the incisions; and the fairies donated their pure crystals to decorate them.

When all the Rings of Light were ready, each kingdom kept one in its custody, as a promise to defend and protect the members of each kingdom against bullies and evildoers.

🔹 🔹 🔹

Unfortunately, many, many years ago, some of the rings were stolen and ended up in the wrong hands. Many evildoers use the rings for war and not for peace.

How to Train a Dragon

I read the writing on the ring. It said "Only for Peace."

As I was leaving the treasure room, I bumped into Sterling. She gasped when she saw the ring on my paw.

"Now that you have a Ring of Light, you must begin your dragon training," she declared.

"Dragon training? I was thinking I might take a quick nap," I squeaked. "Doesn't the salty sea air make you drowsy?"

But Sterling just ignored me.

She dragged me up to the deck as she blew into her flute. Immediately, the Dragon of the Rainbow and Sparkle arrived.

Sterling leafed through the **DRAGON**

TRAINER'S MANUAL.

   LESSON NUMBER ONE: How to care for your dragon!

Hours later I had learned all the ways to care for a dragon.

LESSON NUMBER TWO: Air fighting!

Soon I had learned:

How to **TAKE OFF**!

How to **land**!

How to do crazy **acrobatics**!

And even how to do some special moves to use in a battle!

Turn the page to read Sterling's manual.

The *Dragon of the Rainbow* really liked the acrobatics lesson. "**YEEE-HAAAWWW!**" he cried. "Are we having fun or what?!"

I didn't have the energy to answer. My whiskers trembled with fright and my stomach lurched.

THE SECRET ART OF DRAGON TRAINING

Are you ready to become a perfect dragon trainer? With these short lessons you will learn all the techniques for taking care of and riding your dragon. You will also learn how to take some small but necessary precautions.

❋ LESSON NUMBER ONE ❋
HOW TO CARE FOR YOUR DRAGON!

SADDLE THE DRAGON

It is a simple but delicate operation. If you don't want to fall flat on the ground, remember to pull the straps tight. And above all, try to do it quickly: Dragons have very, very, very little patience!

Teeth Brushing

Proper dental hygiene is very important!

Nail Filing

Keep your dragon's paws perfectly manicured.

Food...

Dragons eat large quantities of food, and it has to be very, very spicy!

...And Digestion!

A good dragon owner always cleans up a dragon's messes!

A Warning!

Never, ever walk past the back paws of your dragon!

Ughhh...

1

Finally, the *Dragon* landed.

I tumbled off him, clutching my paw to my mouth. I raced across the deck.

My stomach **FLIPPED** and **FLOPPED**!

Help...

2

I barely made it to the side of the ship before I got sick. Poor me!

I hoped that the training was over. Anyone could see I was a **total** mess. But Sterling just opened her book and continued.

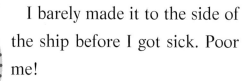

...Bleeck!

3

"Okay, Knight. Let's get started on **Lesson Number Three**: How to use the *Ring of Light*," she said.

I stood up. "Um, Sterling,

maybe we can do this another time. I'm really not feeling so hot," I began.

But just then I heard a loud clatter. I looked up to find **Thunderhorn** trotting toward me.

He looked me right in the eyes. "We are here to save Blossom, Knight," he said seriously. "You must pull yourself together. Now, are you or are you not ready to be a true **Keeper of the Ring**?"

I blinked. A true **Keeper of the Ring**? What did that mean? It all sounded very serious and a little bit **scary**. But then I thought of Blossom, and I nodded.

"I guess I'm ready," I squeaked.

Thunderhorn stamped his hoof. "Don't **guess**, always **know**!"

he insisted. "Now, before Sterling teaches you to **fight** with the ring, you need to make it **radiate** light."

I gulped. "How do I d-d-do that?" I stammered. "Do I press a **BUTTON**?"

Thunderhorn roared with laughter. What was it with this deer? One minute he was **YELLING** at me, and the next minute he was LAUGHING his antlers off.

Suddenly, Thunderhorn grew still. "To make the sword of light appear, you must CLEAR your mind of every **FEAR**. Let your heart be peaceful. And most of all, have faith in yourself!" he said.

I tried to do as Thunderhorn instructed, but it wasn't easy to forget all my fears. Did I mention that I'm a total SCAREDY-MOUSE?

Every day we were on the ship, I practiced and practiced.

Then, finally, one night, a sword of the

WHITEST LIGHT radiated from the ring! My heart filled with *hope* and **joy**.

Sterling still needed to teach me how to fly a dragon, but at that moment, I felt **PURE STRENGTH**.

We would save Blossom — I was sure of it!

LONG LIVE THE QUEEN!!!

good will triumph! good will triumph!

In the Scary
Land of
Nightmares

WELCOME TO THE LAND OF NIGHTMARES!

For the rest of the trip, Sterling taught me how to fight with the *ring*. Around us, the sky was becoming more and more **smoky**. The air was more and more **UNBREATHABLE**. And we were all feeling more and more **hopeless**.

At dawn on the seventh day, Horizon threw down the anchor in the **GULF OF SAD AWAKENINGS**. We got off the boat at **Shiver Beach**.

Suddenly, there were **THUNDER** and *lightning* and **rain**. We had obviously entered the **LAND OF NIGHTMARES!**

Ghosts Ghosts

Calligram: words positioned so they form a picture

THE LAND OF NIGHTMARES

Many years ago the Land of Nightmares was called the KINGDOM OF DREAMS. It was a beautiful place governed by a good and wise king. But the Queen of the Witches placed an evil spell on the land, transforming it into an ugly place with a cold and nasty king.

The Royal Palace was dug from a volcano and contains a terrible prison, the PIT OF SIGHS.

The King of Nightmares is Grim the Grouch. He is the half brother of Cackle, the Queen of the Witches. He is also called the Lord of Fright and He Who Wears the Rock Mask. The reason Grim wears the rock mask is that Cackle tricked him. The mask is bewitched, and Cackle convinced him to wear it by telling him that his kingdom would last only as long as he hid his face.

The Land of Nightmares does not have a queen, because Grim has never been in love. He is afraid of good feelings and positive emotions.

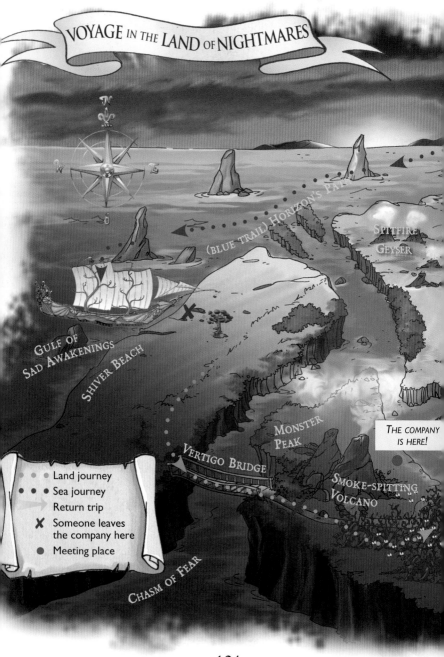

VOYAGE IN THE LAND OF NIGHTMARES

(BLUE TRAIL) HORIZON'S PA...

SPITFIRE
GEYSER

GULF OF
SAD AWAKENINGS

SHIVER BEACH

MONSTER
PEAK

THE COMPANY
IS HERE!

VERTIGO BRIDGE

SMOKE-SPITTING
VOLCANO

Land journey
Sea journey
Return trip
Someone leaves
the company here
Meeting place

CHASM OF FEAR

THRONE
OF POWER

VOLCANO
OF NIGHTMARES

DESERT OF FIRE AND ICE

PRICKLY FOREST

HAUNTED
LAKE

WHISPERING
WOODS

PANIC LAKE

BRUISE

LAGOON

SLOBBER SWAMP

ANXIETY PLATEAU

CASTLE OF
OLD DREAMS

STENCH FOREST

RIVER OF LOST MEMORIES

WHO LEFT FISH BONES IN MY HAT?

We left Horizon docked in front of **Shiver Beach*** and set up camp for the night.

I snacked on Queen Cozy's sugar cookies. Crunch! Crunch! Crunch! They were whisker-licking good!

Strongheart munched on raw onions, and Gray ate fish.

I checked the **COMPASS** to make sure we were going in the right direction.

Suddenly, **STRONGHEART** picked something out of his hat.

Who was it?

* Follow their travels on the map on pages 124–125.

"Who left **FISH BONES** in my **HAT**?" he roared.

Strongheart waved his hat in the air. "I know it was you, you rotten **fur ball**!" he thundered, chasing **GRAY** across the beach.

Gray took off like a shot. He climbed up an oak tree and began throwing acorns at Strongheart.

"Listen, **big nose**, you couldn't catch me if I gave you **ten** head starts! You're so **SLOW** you make my **great-grandma Creaky** look fast!" Gray shrieked.

Strongheart was enraged. He shook the trunk of the tree and glared up at Gray. "**Fish face!**" he shouted. "**Onion breath!**" Gray shouted back.

I tried to stop them, but it was no use. They wouldn't listen.

Finally, Thunderhorn stepped forward and said just one word: "**Enough!**"

His voice was so **loud** and so **firm** everyone stopped.

"You should be ASHAMED of yourselves. We promised to support each other. We are a company and we have a mission. There must be peace between us," Thunderhorn said.

Strongheart's face turned **red** from shame. "Um, so sorry, GRaY. I really shouldn't have called you **FUR BALL** or fish face or . . . ," he began.

Gray interrupted him. "I get the idea, Strongheart," he purred. "And I'm sorry I said you were slower than Grandma Creaky. She can barely make it to the litter box!"

GOOD-BYE, HORIZON!

At **dawn** the next day, we were all ready to continue our journey. Unfortunately, Horizon had to say good-bye to us.

"If only I could **walk**," she said sadly. "I would *love* to come with you. But I guess that's the downside of living on the **WATER**. Oh, well. What can you do, right?"

I patted her deck. "It's okay," I said. "We will tell the queen what you did to save her." Then Horizon gave me a beautiful **pearl** to give Blossom as a gift.

THE SHIP'S PEARL

Sparkle — Sterling's Silver Dragon — and the *Dragon of the Rainbow* stayed behind to protect Horizon.

"BE CAREFUL!" I called as we headed off. "We'll be back soon."

GOOD-BYE, STRONGHEART!

It seemed that we were walking for ages. It was *sad* to travel in that **DARK** land, where we would surely encounter some trolls.

We arrived at the CHASM OF FEAR. We had to cross the chasm on a **shaky** bridge, but Strongheart was too **BIG**. He lengthened his step to leap over the ravine, but he *TRIPPED* and his boot got stuck! He tried to get it out, but it wouldn't **BUDGE**.

"Come on, you big **lug**!" Gray shouted. "You can do it!"

"It's stuck, you **fuzzy feline**!" Strongheart complained.

Finally, we pulled his foot out, but Strongheart's boot was **STUCK** for good.

"Guess I'll need to hit the shoe store when I get home," he sighed.

Strongheart began walking, but his big bare foot hurt from stepping on rocks. He was moving very **SLOWLY**.

When we arrived at the Smoke-spitting Volcano, there was so much smoke we could barely breathe. Tears streamed from our eyes.

The thick clouds of smoke that were filling the **Kingdom of Fantasy** were coming from the Smoke-spitting Volcano in the **LAND OF NIGHTMARES**! That explains why the sunlight couldn't heat up the land, and why it was so **cold** that winter had returned.

Strongheart glared up at the volcano. "Enough with this smoke, and this **cold** and this STINK! I am strong! I will turn off this volcano!"

Gray rolled his eyes. "You can barely walk, big boy," he snickered. "What are you going to do?"

"Come on, you two," I insisted. "No more bickering. We need to SAVE Blossom!"

Strongheart hung his head. "I hate to admit it, but Gray is right," he said sadly. "I can't put out the volcano, and I'm SLOWING you down. I'd better leave."

We all tried to convince him to stay, but he took a feather from his hat. "Bring this to the queen," he said. "Tell her it's a gift from Strongheart."

"Don't worry, Strongheart. We will tell her all about how you helped to save her," I said. Then we all hugged him and told him to wait for us by the Smoke-spitting Volcano.

THE GIANT'S FEATHER

GOOD-BYE, PUSS IN BOOTS!

We began walking without **STRONGHEART**. I really missed my **gigantic friend**! I noticed that GRAY missed him, too, though he tried not to show it.

"Good thing we **LOST** that **BIG LUG**," he mumbled. "He was really **dragging** us down." Then he let out a **sad meow**.

We passed by the **Stench Forest**, which was surrounded by a cloud of flies.

Then we found ourselves in front of the tremendous *River of Lost Memories*.

The water in the river formed dangerous **waterfalls** and *whirlpools*. Only those who really knew how to swim well would be able to cross it.

"Well, it looks like we have no choice. There are no bridges, so we will have to **swim** across the river," I told the others.

Gray turned pale. "**Swim?**" he meowed. "You mean jump in the water? Get our fur *wet*? Not on your life! I mean, I'll do anything, but I **CANNOT** swim — I'm a **CAT**! Sorry, Knight, but I am afraid I'm going to have to stay behind."

Then he looked behind him and sighed. "If only **STRONGHEART** were here. He could have put me on his shoulders. I wouldn't have had to get one paw wet."

The cat pulled out one of his whiskers and slipped it into a pendant.

"Take this whisker to the queen and tell her that it is a gift from GRAY," he said.

I hugged him and said good-bye. "Don't worry. I will make sure to tell the queen what you did to help save her," I said. "Wait for us at the Smoke-spitting Volcano."

THE CAT'S WHISKER

GOOD-BYE, SILVER DRAGON PRINCESS!

Now Thunderhorn, King of the Elves; Sterling, Princess of the Silver Dragons; and I, *Sir Geronimo of Stilton* or, er, Geronimo Stilton, were the only three left.

We crossed through one **SCARY** place after another. I was so afraid, my teeth were **chattering** up a storm. It felt like every minute we were losing another member of the company!

We had just passed the **Slobber Swamp** when a giant serpent emerged from the **slimy** water. He had only one eye and teeth as **SHARP** as knives. **Gulp!**

The monster hissed threateningly, slithering toward us and leaving behind him a trail of gooey, sticky **slime**.

SLOBBERY SERPENT SLIME

IT'S GOOEY! IT'S STICKY!

IT'S SLIME!

The serpent **BLOCKED** our path to prevent us from continuing. Now how would we get through?

"I have an idea," Sterling said. "I will stay here and distract this **FEROCIOUS CREATURE** while the rest of you continue on your way."

She took her **SILVER FLUTE** out of her satchel.

"Please take this to the queen and tell her it's a gift from the Silver Dragon Princess," she said.

She hugged us.

Then she pointed her *SWORD* at the serpent. "**Back off!**" she commanded.

The serpent glared at Thunderhorn and me as we slipped passed him. **Cheese sticks**, he was slimy!

"Wait for us at the Smoke-spitting Volcano!" I yelled back to Sterling. "And thank you!"

GOOD-BYE, KING THUNDERHORN!

Now there were only two of us left. How could we save Blossom with only **TWO** members of the company? I tried not to panic. I mean, it could be **worse**. At least I had **Thunderhorn** by my side.

We crossed through the Whispering Woods and entered the PRICKLY FOREST.

I wondered why they called the forest PRICKLY. After a few short steps, I understood.

YOUCH! There were **thorns** everywhere!

As we walked, the thorns become more and more pointy.

Thunderhorn's long horns kept getting caught in **TANGLES** of thorns.

His steps grew slower and slower and **slower**. Finally, he stopped. "I am sorry, *Sir Knight,*

but I cannot continue. I'm slowing you down too much," he said.

My jaw dropped. This couldn't be happening! I was too much of a scaredy-mouse to continue all alone!

I did everything I could think of to keep Thunderhorn by my side.

First I gave him one of Queen Cozy's **cookies** to build up his **strength**.

Then I used the *Ring of Light* to clear a path, cutting the largest, most PRICKLY branches away from his horns.

But it was no use.

Thunderhorn was too exhausted to continue.

"I appreciate all you have done, Sir Knight," he said. "But you've got to take it from here."

Then he took off the pendant he wore around his neck.

THE DEER'S PENDANT

"Give this to the queen and tell her it is a gift from **Thunderhorn, King of the Elves**," he instructed.

I hugged him. I felt so **sad**. It was as if I had just lost my last friend.

"Wait for me at the Smoke-spitting Volcano," I said, waving good-bye.

ALL ALONE IN THE DEEP, DARK WOODS

As I trudged along, I noticed something GLIMMERING in the sky. It was a full moon. I don't know why, but for some reason, seeing the moon made me feel even LONELIER.

Oh, how did I get myself into this mess? I thought. I was **all alone** in the DEEP, DARK WOODS!

I started to shiver. Then I twisted my tail in a knot. Ouch!

I was so miserable I began to cry, but the cold turned my tears to ice.

plink! plink! plink! plink!
plink! plink! plink! plink!

I decided it was time for a cookie break.

I **gobbled** the last one up and felt much better.

I'm not sure what it is about Queen Cozy's **cookies**, but they always make me feel **warm** inside. Maybe it's the fact that she makes them with so much *love*.

I licked my whiskers, then checked the compass.

It was pointing north, toward the **VOLCANO OF NIGHTMARES**.

I looked north and saw the **VOLCANO OF NIGHTMARES**. It was shining in the moonlight and was so **TALL** that the top poked through the clouds.

How would I ever **CLiMB** it?

At that moment, a scroll slid out of my bag. It was Scribblehopper's **poem**. That frog is a terrible poet, but this poem really made me **SMILE**.

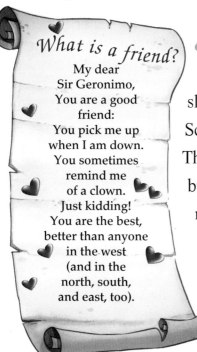

What is a friend?

My dear
Sir Geronimo,
You are a good
friend:
You pick me up
when I am down.
You sometimes
remind me
of a clown.
Just kidding!
You are the best,
better than anyone
in the west
(and in the
north, south,
and east, too).

In the Palace
of the King
of Nightmares

I looked north and saw the Volcano of Nightmares.

IT'S ALL UP TO YOU!

I CLIMBED and CLIMBED and CLIMBED. It was so DARK! Did I mention I'm afraid of the dark, and of SPIDERS, and of COTTON BALLS? With the last of my energy, I climbed to the top of the volcano.

My paws were slipping on the ice, and my snout was frozen over with icicles.

I took one step forward and THREE steps backward. The whole time I was TERRIFIED. What if I . . . fellllllllllllllllllllllllllllll?!

I tried giving myself a pep talk. *SNAP OUT OF IT*, Geronimo, I told myself. *You have to save Blossom! It's all up to YOU! You, you, YOU!*

When that didn't work, I tried thinking about  happy things, like **chocolate-covered cheesy chews**, my nephew BENJAMIN, and my great-aunt Ratsy's cozy comforter. Finally, I arrived at the top of the volcano.

I stayed there for a moment, my heart pounding from all that exercise. I really needed to work out more!

Then I looked around.

There was **snow** everywhere, but the dazzling whiteness was interrupted by thousands of *FIERY* volcanoes!

AN ELEVATOR . . . OF NIGHTMARES!

I explored the top of the volcano. It was **flat** and **snowcapped**. It looked like a cake covered in **frosting**.

At the center of it was an **ENORMOUSE** throne made out of **STONE**.

Strange. How would I get into the palace?

I was breathless from the climb, so I sat down on the throne to rest for a bit.

How odd!

The stone was **WARM**.

Then it started to vibrate and move! I tried not to scream. The throne was some sort of **bizarre** elevator.

I was being **sucked** into the volcano!

Oh, when would this nightmare end?

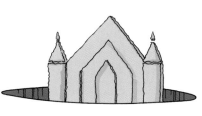

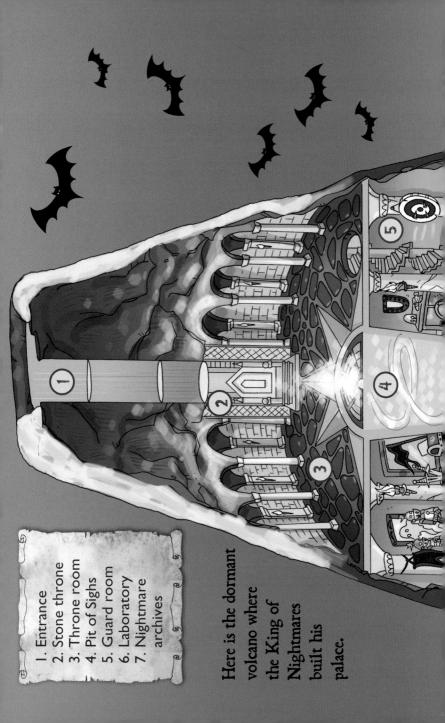

1. Entrance
2. Stone throne
3. Throne room
4. Pit of Sighs
5. Guard room
6. Laboratory
7. Nightmare archives

Here is the dormant volcano where the King of Nightmares built his palace.

THE PALACE OF THE KING OF NIGHTMARES

FEELING HOT, HOT, HOT!

The throne descended **farther** and **farther**, through a long and **DARK** tunnel, until it stopped in an **ENORMOUSE** round room that had been dug from rock.

I got off the throne and looked around, **ASTONISHED**. Everything was made of **ROCK** — the walls, the floor, and even the ceiling.

AND IT WAS HOT!

It seemed like I was in an oven!

I brushed against the walls. Even they were **HOT**!

Then I remembered something: I was inside a **VOLCANO**!

Behind me was the throne, and in front of me

* You can find the Fantasian Alphabet on page 291.

TRY TO DECIPHER THE WRITING!*

was a tiny window with a balcony. There were **MASSIVE** stone columns along the balcony, and there was a pit covered by a metal grate shaped like a spiderweb in the center of the room.

There was writing around the edge of the pit. It said *Pit of Sighs* in Fantasian.

For some reason, I began to feel very sad. I sighed and sighed and sighed.

Suddenly, I smelled a faint scent of *roses*. Then I heard a faint song.

It was coming from the center of the room.

I got closer and the scent of roses became more **iNTENSE**.

I **stretched** out to look into the pit and the scent of *roses* became even stronger!

The pit was **dark**, like a sewer rat's favorite vacation hangout. But I spotted a *glimmer* of blue way **DOWN** at the very bottom of the pit!

Suddenly, I recognized her.

"BLOSSOOOOMMMMM!" I squeaked without thinking.

Oops! Had anyone heard me?

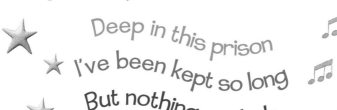

Deep in this prison
I've been kept so long
But nothing can hide
The joy in my song . . .

BLOSSOOOOMMMMM!

Oops!

I Tried and I
Tried . . .

I pushed my snout against the grate on top of the pit. "**your Majesty!**" I called. "How are you?"

"Who is it?" the queen answered warily.

I told her who I was and that I had come to rescue her. Of course, I explained about the entire FANTASY COMPANY and how we had all worked together to find her.

"In fact, everyone gave me gifts for you," I said. Then I tried to lift the metal grate. But it was so, so, so **heavy**!

Ughhhh!

I tried and I tried with all my strength but didn't move the grate even an inch!

Then I heard **footsteps** approaching.

"Hurry, get out of here!" the queen cried. "Don't put yourself in danger because of me!"

I hid behind a column.

Who was arriving?

WHO? **WHO??** **WHO???**

STRENGTH AND POWER TO GRIM!

A troop of STONE SOLDIERS entered and positioned themselves around the *Pit of Sighs*.

Their leader looked down. "The Queen of the Fairies is still our prisoner! Everything is all right!"

The soldiers beat their lances against their shields, producing a deafening sound.

Clang! Clang! Clang!

"**STRENGTH** and **power** to Grim, KING OF NIGHTMARES, the Lord of the Stone Mask!" the leader shouted.

The soldiers hit their lances against their shields.

Clang! Clang! Clang!

"Thanks to Grim, we will **RULE** over the entire Kingdom of Fantaaassssyyyyyyyyyyy!"

Clang! Clang! Clang!

With that, the STONE SOLDIERS swiveled

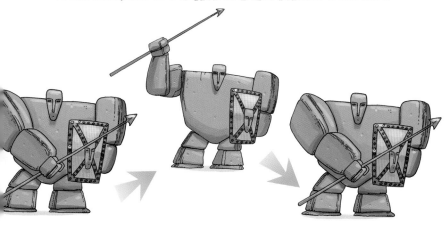

on their heels and marched out of the throne room.

As soon as the sounds of their footsteps vanished, I snuck out from behind the column.

Thank goodness they were gone! All that CLANGING was giving me a giant headache!

I ran toward the grate that enclosed the *Pit of Sighs* and began to pull on it again, but suddenly, I heard more noisy footsteps.

Rats! Who was it this time?

WHO? WHO?? WHO???

THREE BATS, A
SKUNK . . . AND A
SCORPION!

A **TALL, THIN** female figure entered the room. She was holding a candlestick in the shape of a **bat**. She had **LONG RED** hair. Her eyes were almond shaped and were two **DIFFERENT** COLORS. She was wearing silk slippers. I recognized her right away. She was beautiful, but her treacherous stare was pure **evil**.

She put her face up to the *Pit of Sighs* and let out a terrible cackle.

I turned pale. It was none other than 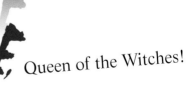 Queen of the Witches!

Bumble

Humphrey

Chubby

Smelly

Stingy

"Finally, you are in my power!" she laughed.

The witch was accompanied by three **bats**, one **SKUNK**, and one **scorpion**.

She sniffed the air. "I smell a rat!" she cried.

The three bats yelled, "The witch smells a rat!"

I thought I would faint from **FRIGHT**. They were about to find me! But then Cackle yelled, "Who made that terrible stink?"

The scorpion pointed to the skunk. "He did it!" he said accusingly.

I stink . . . because I'm a skunk!

The bats **flapped** their wings. "He did it! He did it!" they repeated.

Cackle shrieked, "Enough! You bats are driving me crazy, and that stink is making me gag! Let's go!"

As soon as they left, I slipped out of hiding.

But before I could get back to the Pit of Sighs, I heard **more** footsteps! I hid behind the column again.

Who was it this time?

WHO? WHO?? WHO???

GRIM THE GROUCH

Another troop of stone soldiers marched in with heavy steps.

THUMP THUMP THUMP!

The soldiers were carrying a chair with closed drapes across it.

The leader of the soldiers yelled, "Pay respect to the **KING OF NIGHTMARES!**"

I watched as one foot, *elegantly* dressed in a black leather boot, emerged from behind the drapes. Then I saw the hem of his **silk** black coat. Finally, he got out of the chair and moved toward the throne.

He turned around. Instead of his face, all I saw was a **STONE MASK!**

Have you ever seen someone wearing a mask

made of STONE? Let me tell you, it is a very CREEPY sight! All I could make out were the king's eyes behind the mask. They looked SAD. His long **black** hair was tied in a ponytail, and I noticed a large RING on his finger.

The king clapped and pointed to the pit.

The stone soldiers lifted the BLACK GRATE and pulled Blossom out of the pit.

Then the king clapped his hands again. The soldiers left.

The king clapped and pointed to Blossom. Cheese niblets, this king was clap-happy! I was still thinking about all that clapping when the king's voice boomed like thunder.

"I, Grim the Grouch, King of Nightmares, order you to sing me a fairy song!" he commanded.

I Like Being Evil . . .

I frowned. Didn't anyone ever say **PLEASE** anymore? What happened to asking Ní(eⱢⲨ? The king really needed to learn some *manners*. I mean, who orders someone to **SiNG** for them? It was just downright **RUDE**!

But Blossom didn't seem to notice the king's behavior. Or maybe she was just too polite to say anything.

Instead, she began to sing in the most *beautiful* voice:

> *See the good in every heart.*
> *Make a brand-new joyful start.*
> *If evil is your only friend,*
> *You'll never have a happy end.*

The king brushed a **tear** from his **EYE**.

Then he jumped to his feet.

"That's **ENOUGH**!" he cried. "Your words are **CONFUSING** me. I am the King of Nightmares. I don't have time for **GOODNESS** and **JOY**. And besides, I **like** being evil . . . I think."

He shook his head and watched as Blossom began to dance.

She twirled with grace and poise. She reminded me of a **DELICATE** flower swaying in the breeze.

As the king watched her dance, tears began to pour from his **EYES**. Then the most **AMAZING** thing happened — his mask began to **crack**!

"I can't **believe** it!" he gasped. "I'm cracking up! I mean, I'm not cracking up in a **bad** way. I'm cracking up in a **good** way. I can **feel** things again!"

The fairy smiled.

"I knew you could do it," she whispered.

Goodness makes you happy!!!

Goodness makes you happy!!!

Evil dries you up. . . .

Goodness makes you happy!!!

Goodness makes you happy!!!

Goodness makes you happy!!!

THE DARK FORCES

Suddenly, the door burst open. The Queen of the Witches strode in.

"So much for that **HAPPY ENDING**," I muttered. Then I clapped my paw over my mouth.

"SSSssssssilENCE!"

Cackle shrieked.

"Half Brother, pull yourself together!" she said to the king. "My dark forces are ready to take over the Kingdom of Fantasy, but I need your thousand **STONE SOLDIERS**. Where are they? They're **MiSSiNG**!"

Then Cackle looked out the window.

THE FORCES OF DARKNESS

WITCHES: These evil creatures are jealous of the fairies, and they especially dislike Blossom!

OGRES: They are big, fat, and ferocious, especially when they are hungry . . . which is always!

LITTLE OGRES: They are small, agile, evil, and cowardly.

HEARTLESS KNIGHTS: These empty suits of armor are completely under Cackle's control!

STONE SOLDIERS: There are one thousand of these strong, massive, invincible soldiers!

TROLLS: They are ugly, smelly, and armed with enormous clubs!

PUT THE FAIRY BACK!

As soon as the **DARK FORCES** had gathered at the foot of the **VOLCANO OF NIGHTMARES**, Cackle stepped out on the balcony and made a speech. Then she turned to her half brother.

"Put the fairy back in the *Pit of Sighs*!" Cackle commanded Grim.

Grim was silent.

Cackle's face grew **red** with anger. She really

On guard, Half Brother!

I don't want to fight anymore!

How dare you?

That's enough with the magic!

needed to learn to take some DEEP breaths, but I figured now wasn't the time to tell her.

"GRIM! Get the COTTON out of your ears!" the witch shrieked. "I said throw the fairy in the pit — NOW!"

But Grim just shook his head. And even though I couldn't see his face behind his **mask**, something about him seemed Different.

Throw the fairy in the pit!

No, never!

I've had it with your terrible plots!

"**NO!**" he told Cackle firmly.

The witch flew into a witchy **tantrum**. First she **STAMPED** her feet. Then she **screamed**. Her ring began to **glow** and a sword of **WHITE LIGHT** emerged from it. She smiled evilly. "On guard, Half Brother!" she yelled.

Grim had no **CHOICE** — he had to defend himself. A second later his own *ring* began to **glow**. Now he had his own sword of **WHITE LIGHT**.

The two began to duel.

It was **SUPER-SCARY** to watch. Grim was **STRONG**, but Cackle was **QUICK**.

The swords **ripped** through the air like my uncle Cheesebelly's *ELECTRIC CHEESE SLICER* on high speed.

I tried not to watch, but I couldn't help myself. I had to see who won the fight. Then I noticed

something strange. The king's clothes were slowly changing color. They went from **black** to **blue**.

Could it be he was turning **good**?

Then a **terrible** thing happened. The **WHITE LIGHT** from Cackle's sword hit Grim!

Slowly the King of Nightmares fell

down,

    down,

        down. . . .

As he was falling, his stone mask **cracked** in half and **shattered**. Grim's whole body turned a shimmering blue. I stared in **AMAZEMENT** as transparent fairy wings sprouted on his back.

Was Grim turning into a **fairy**? Was he going to **FLY** away?

FLAP! FLAP! FLAP!

Suddenly, I heard a terrifying **scream**.

The scorpion had pinched Blossom, and she **fainted**.

Then the three bats grabbed her with their **claws** and lifted her up into the air.

Pinch!

Frrrrrr!

Spritzzzzz!

Next **Cackle** ordered the skunk to spray the room with a **disgusting stench**.

It was such an awful smell I was afraid I might **TOSS MY CHEESE**.

The witch ran to the window. Her **BLACK** Dragon was waiting for her outside.

She jumped onto his back, and the bats dropped Blossom onto the dragon right behind Cackle. Then the dragon took off.

Flap flap flap!

CACKLE! CACKLE! CACKLE!

I raced to the window. The witch was getting away and she was taking Blossom with her!

Her evil **LAUGHTER** filled the air.

CACKLE. **CACKLE.** CACKLE. CACKLE.

NO ONE CAN DEFEAT ME,
I'M EVIL AND STRONG.
I'LL FIGHT ALL NIGHT LONG
AND KICK YOU IN THE KNEE.

HEE. HEE. **HEE.** HEE. HEE. HEE. **HEE!**

I rolled my eyes. Cackle's rhymes were as **BAD** as Scribblehopper's!

After Cackle's voice faded away, I knelt beside Grim. He didn't look so *HOT*. In fact, now that he had turned BLUE, he looked really **cold**. Did you know that BLUE is a **cold** color and **red** is a WARM color?

But where was I? Oh yes, **GRIM**. I was staring at him when suddenly I had an idea.

I looked in my bag and found the vial that Queen Cozy had given me.

Quickly, I poured a drop of the liquid on his wound.

It worked like a **CHARM**! Grim's eyes popped open. The dragon tears were already taking effect!

"Thanks for saving me, Sir Knight. But now you'd better go. I'm too weak to fight, and you're

the only one left who can **SAVE** Blossom!" he said.

I chewed my whiskers.

Then I remembered the SILVER FLUTE Sterling had given me.

I went to the balcony and played it.

As quick as lightning, the *Dragon of the Rainbow* appeared.

I grabbed his golden neck, and with a flap of his powerful **wings**, we took off after Cackle.

I tried not to look down as clouds **ZIPPED** past my snout.

Oh, when would I get used to flyyyyyyyyyyyyyyyyyying?!!!!!!!!!!!

Dragons' Duel!

The Black Dragon was already far ahead of us. He was headed south toward the **Kingdom of the Witches**.

I closed my eyes and tried not to think about that **terrifying** place. It was such a DARK and dreary land. And when I say DARK, I mean DARK. That's because it's always nighttime in their kingdom, because the witches

hate **sunlight**. Isn't that **TOTALLY CREEPY**? Everyone knows that **sunlight** makes you happier.

The Dragon of the Rainbow flapped his **wings** with intense concentration. He took advantage of every air pocket, every **GUST** of wind, and every wind **CURRENT**.

UP! DOWN! UP! DOWN!

We were going **SO FAST** I felt like I was

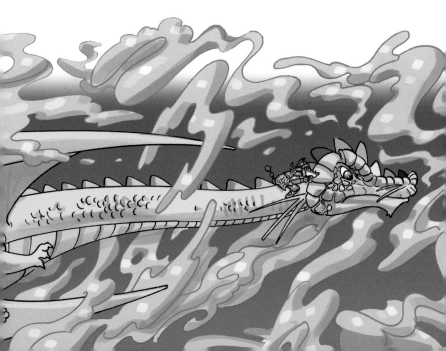

riding the **SCARIEST** roller coaster ever!

Then things got even **SCARIER**.

The Dragon of the Rainbow caught up with the Black Dragon, and the two began to **fight**.

They tossed and turned in midair while I hung on for **DEAR LIFE**!

Oh, how did I get myself into such a mess? I should have been home taking a nice cheddar bubble bath or flying a kite with my nephew Benjamin at **Scampertown Park**.

Instead, I watched in horror as the Black Dragon tried to take a bite out of the Dragon of the Rainbow's **paw**!

The *Dragon of the Rainbow* moved quickly and **STRUCK** the

Black Dragon across the snout with his **golden** tail.

BONK!

I was so busy watching the fight, I didn't notice the witch **FIRING UP** her ring.

The sword of light grazed my snout.

YOUCH!

In a flash, I lit up my own **ring**. Our swords clashed, creating thousands of **SPARKS**!

Luckily, I remembered Sterling's lesson on acrobatic flying. We dove straight **DOWN**.

THE WITCH THOUGHT WE WERE FALLING!

Instead, we stopped in midair. I looked Cackle in the **eye**.

"Cheese niblets!" I squeaked. "Do you know you have an **enormouse pimple** on your nose?"

Cackle was HORRIFIED. She put down her sword and touched her FACE.

"Oh, how MORTIFYING, how EMBARRASSING, how **humiliating**!" she cried.

While she was distracted, I POINTED my sword at the **BLACK DRAGON**.

This is it! I told myself. *You can do it, Geronimo! For* **Blossom**, *for the* FANTASY COMPANY, *and for the gigantic box of* **Cheesy Chews** *you're going to buy yourself when you get home!*

HEY, KNIGHTSY!

Then I struck the Black Dragon so hard it reared **UP** and caused Cackle to fall **DOWN** toward the ground.

Luckily for her, the Black Dragon caught her with his *tail*.

"Hey, Knightsy!" Cackle said to me. "How about we make a deal? You give up and let me keep Blossom, and I'll make you a famouse **MOVIE STAR**! You'll have your name in LIGHTS! Everyone will want your *autograph*! What do you say?"

I shook my head.

"Not interested," I said.

She scratched her head.

"Okay, how about I give you **money**?" she

said, bargaining.

I shook my head.

"JEWELS?"

I shook my head.

"A lifetime supply of **cheese**?"

Okay, I admit it — the cheese was tempting. I mean, just thinking about all the cheesy **pizzas**, mozzarella **milk shakes**, and cream cheese **casseroles** I could make . . . But I'm proud to say that I did the right thing and refused Cackle's offer.

She was **FURIOUS**.

"YOU'LL BE SORRY!!!"

D-D-D-Death?

The witch looked at me with **EVIL** in her eyes.

She lifted her sword. "Now we fight to the **death**!" she screeched.

I blinked. "D-d-d-death?" I stammered. "Can't we just **shake** paws and be friends?"

Cackle ignored me. "On one and two and . . ."

Then, before she hit three, she *attacked*!

But . . . that's not fair!

Take that!

Oww oww oww!

And this!

"Hey! That's not fair!" I protested. "You didn't say 'THREE'!"

But the witch just giggled wickedly. "Only a FOOL would actually believe a **witch** would play fair!" she shouted.

Then she attacked me again.

The two swords of light from our rings crossed, creating a rainfall of blue and white SPARKS.

I felt **dazed** and tired. If only I could rest for just a minute or . . .

And take this!

Oh, poor me!

Ooohhh . . .

And here!

At that moment, Cackle's sword **swished** by, just inches from my whiskers. **Holey cheese!**

I **SNAPPED** to attention. I thought of Blossom and her ᵍᵉⁿ†ᴸᵉ smile. I thought of the Kingdom of the Fairies, frozen by Cackle's evil spell and covered in **ice**. Finally, I thought of all my friends in the FANTASY COMPANY.

How could I let them **DOWN**? With my last bit of **STRENGTH**, I hit Cackle with my sword of light.

At last, the Queen of the Witches was defeated!

The bats carried Cackle away. And even though I heard her muttering as she left, I knew the witch was done **FIGHTING** . . . for now.

I was so proud of myself I did a little dance. Then I shouted,

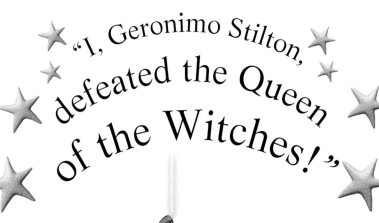

"I, Geronimo Stilton, defeated the Queen of the Witches!"

THANK YOU,
SIR GERONIMO

I was so **exhausted** after my battle with Cackle I could barely move.

Did I mention I'm not much of a sportsmouse? Luckily, the *Dragon of the Rainbow* took care of me. He grabbed my suit of armor between his teeth and placed me on his back.

Then he picked up Blossom, too. Once we were all settled, the dragon took off. We soared high into the clouds. Normally, I would have been gnawing on my pawnails or reciting my A B C's to calm my nerves. Oh, how I hate to **fly**! But this time I was so tired I just closed my eyes. Soon, I was snoring *peacefully*, nestled between the dragon's wings.

We even stopped to pick up Grim along the way. I was so exhausted I just kept on snoring. **How embarrassing!**

We flew all day and all night for three days in a row. Once I regained my strength, I chatted with Blossom about my crazy adventures with the FANTASY COMPANY. And I was finally able to give her the **Gifts** from my friends.

At dawn on the third day, we arrived at the meeting spot, the Smoke-spitting Volcano. Down below, my friends were running around in circles, waVing wildly. I chuckled. They looked like they were doing some sort of WACKY happy dance! Finally, the Dragon of the Rainbow landed, kicking up a cloud of dust.

Blossom thanked us one by one. "Thank you, POWERFUL Strongheart. Thank you, clever Gray. Thank you, COURAGEOUS Sterling. Thank you, wise Thunderhorn. And most of all, thank you, Sir Geronimo, the BRAVEST knight of all!" she declared.

I turned as red as a tomato.

Bravest knight of all? I was afraid of my own SHADOW! And what about small elevators, DARK closets, and ticking egg timers? They were positively teeth-chattering!

But I figured now wasn't the time to mention it. And besides, there was still one more thing we needed to do — stop the Smoke-spitting Volcano!

The Smoke-spitting Volcano!

LET'S DO THIS THING!

The next morning, the *Dragon of the Rainbow* took the queen and Grim to **Shiver Beach**. Horizon and the Silver Dragon were waiting there.

Meanwhile, the rest of us got ready to climb the Smoke-spitting Volcano. Thunderhorn stamped his hooves. Sterling clutched her arrows. Strongheart did some knee bends. And Gray patted his whiskers and yelled, "Let's do this thing!"

We began to climb ever so **slowly**.

The volcano rumbled.

I tried not to panic.

So I was climbing up a volcano. So it was spitting out flames. There was no reason to get upset.

At last we reached the top.

My muscles **ACHED**. I hadn't done this much exercise since the time I trained for the Mouse

Island Marathon! Plus the **BLACK** soot was making me cough.

In the center of the volcano was a stairway that went

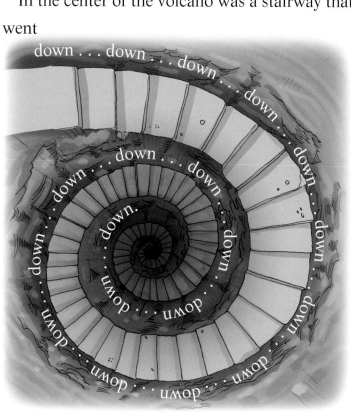

HOTTER THAN A COOKING POT!

Slowly, we made our way down the stairs. My paws were trembling so much I kept tripping. *Get a grip, Geronimo*, I told myself. I was afraid if I didn't stop shaking, I'd end up tumbling snoutfirst the rest of the way. And who knew what terrible **MONSTER** might be waiting for us down below!

Was it an enormous FIRE-BREATHING DRAGON? Another evil witch? Or maybe it was a three-headed CREATURE with teeth like daggers and a taste for mice!

When we arrived at the bottom of the stairs, we found ourselves in a stone corridor. The HEAT was unbearable. Sweat dripped down my fur.

At the end of the hall, there was a **stone door**.

I put my paws against the door to open it.

Bad idea!

I burned my paws!

"**OOOOOOOOOUUUUUUUUUUCH!**" I squeaked.

Then I covered my mouth with one paw. What if someone had heard me???

Just then we heard the strangest noise:

PHEEEEEWWW! PHEEEEWWWW! PHEEEEWWWW!

Oooouuuuuuuch!

Oops!

It almost sounded like someone **breathing** very loudly.

Together we managed to push the door open without getting BURNED.

We found ourselves in an enormouse dark circular room. I felt like we were standing inside a COOKING POT! In a corner was a giant stove, where an immense fire was burning.

Next to the fire, there were bellows. Do you know what bellows are? They're used to **blow** on a fire to make it burn more.

The bellows were as **LARGE** as a bus! Who could possibly use them?

BEATRICE BIGFOOT

Suddenly, from the shadows, a huge hand popped out, with fingers as big as **gas** **pipes**! The hand was working the bellows, **UP** and **DOWN** and **UP** and **DOWN** and **UP** and **DOWN**.

I gulped.

Who did this **GIANT** hand belong to?

Then an arm popped out of the shadows. It was as big as a **mover's truck**! Then a foot popped out. It was as big as an **18-WHEELER**! And finally an enormous face emerged. It was as round and large as a **full moon**!

I twisted my tail in a knot. Who was this giant creature?

The face stared into the FIRE. It was then that I noticed a thick plume of gray smoke.

The smoke rose up the volcano. It billowed out into the sky. So that was what was **PoLLuting** the Kingdom of Fantasy!

Why would someone want to destroy such a **beautiful** place?

I was so annoyed I leaped up and yelled, "**STOP!**"

Then I chewed my whiskers. Maybe yelling at a giant as big as a **house** wasn't the smartest thing to do. In fact, I'd say that on a scale of **one** to **SMART**, it was about a negative three. But instead of **squashing** me like a bug, the giant started crying.

When I looked closer, I saw that the giant was a **WOMAN**.

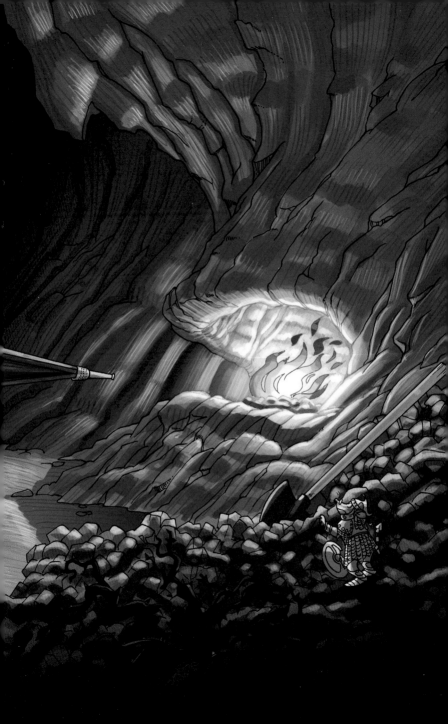

I looked closer at the giant. Her face was caked with dirt and her hair was **WiLD**. Her feet were bare and her clothes were ripped. Even worse, there were f l e a s swarming all around her!

Then I saw an enormouse **ball and chain** around her ankle. Someone was keeping her **PRISONER**!

The giant blew her nose into her sleeve. **HONK!**

I pretended not to notice. After all, I couldn't loan her a tissue. It would be way too *TINY* for her.

"Sorry for all the **blubbering**. It's been a while since I've had company," she sighed. "My name is Beatrice Bigfoot. I used to be the Queen of the Southern Giants until I was captured by trolls."

The Troll People

They live underground in dirty and smelly caves. They are so stinky that you can smell them from miles away. When they prepare to fight, they bang loudly on their drums.

BEAKY VON TROLL — SCIENTIST

LADDER VON TROLL — FIREMAN

STITCHES VON TROLL — DOCTOR

BUTCH VON TROLL — NEWSPAPER DELIVERER

DRUM-DE-DRUM-DRUM!

Just then I heard a horrible noise.

DRUM-DE-DRUM-DRUM! DRUM-DE-DRUM-DRUM! DRUM-DE-DRUM-DRUM! DRUM-DE-DRUM-DRUM! DRUM-DE-DRUM-DRUM! DRUM-DE-DRUM-DRUM!

It was the noise of the trolls' drums.

Then I smelled their terrible **STINK**.

I was **shaking** from head to tail. I remembered the **disgusting** trolls from my first visit to the Kingdom of Fantasy.

Beatrice wrung her hands.

"Oh, no! The **TROLLS** are coming! Cackle ordered them to chain me up. I'm to keep the fire going day and night . . . or else!" She gulped.

I shook my head. Talk about not loving your **day** (and **night**) job!

"Quick!" I told Strongheart. "You've got to

help Beatrice!" Strongheart tugged and pulled at the chain around Beatrice's ankle.

"Come on, you **BIG LUG**!" Gray encouraged the giant. "You can do it!"

At that moment, there was a loud **SNAP**! The chain broke in two. Beatrice was **free**! She showed us a door that led to the outside. Strongheart ran out first and returned with his hat filled with **snow**. When he put out the fire, we all cheered: "**HOORAY!**"

SNAP!

Then we all raced outside. Crumbling cheese crispies! The stinky **TROLLS** were all around us! With another **BANG** of their annoying drums, they **attacked**.

But Strongheart was so mad at the trolls for chaining up Beatrice, he roared with **fury**. Then he sent the trolls flying one by one until they all ended up in a huge **stinky** heap!

THE SECRET
TO BEAUTY

Beatrice shyly thanked Strongheart for his help.

"It was my pleasure," said Strongheart with a bow. "I'm so glad to meet you. I thought I was the only big **GIANT** left in the kingdom. I mean, not that you're extra-**big** or anything. After all, we're all **big**, since we're giants, that is . . . What I mean is . . ."

Gray rolled his eyes. "You'll have to excuse my friend," he told Beatrice. "He doesn't get out much."

The giant shot him a look. I could tell they were about to start arguing.

"Why don't we all welcome **Beatrice** to the company?" I said. "She can come with us to the **Kingdom of the Fairies**."

BEATRICE BIGFOOT

Everyone agreed Beatrice should join us. We left immediately for **Shiver Beach**, where Horizon was docked and **Blossom** and **GRIM** were also waiting.

During the trip, I noticed that the two giants were inseparable. They chatted away like they'd known each other for years.

Plus, they both couldn't stop *smiling*. When we passed a field of flowers, Strongheart reached out and picked a BoUQUeT for Beatrice.

Well, actually it wasn't a bouquet of flowers — it was a bouquet of flowering trees!

Finally, we arrived at **Shiver Beach**. Blossom and Grim waved hello as we approached. I noticed that Grim was looking very blue. Not blue like the **SAD** kind of blue. He was lit up in a **BLUE LIGHT**, just like the Queen of the Fairies.

Before we boarded the ship, Strongheart pulled two golden crowns from his bag. Then he turned to Beatrice. "This is the crown of the King of the Giants. But for a long time, I have been carrying another one around with me. It is a crown fit for a queen. I would like for you to have it."

THE CROWN OF THE KING OF THE GIANTS

THE CROWN OF THE QUEEN OF THE GIANTS

Beatrice smiled. She tried to wipe the **soot** off her face and fix her *hair*, but it was no use.

"Oh, Strongheart," she sighed. "Let's face it — I don't look like a **QUEEN**."

Strongheart disagreed. "You're beautiful," he insisted.

"No, I'm not," Beatrice replied. She blushed a **bright pink**.

"Yes, you are."

"No, I'm not."

"Yes, you are."

Finally, Gray grabbed the **crown** and plunked it on Beatrice's head. "Please take it. You two are driving me crazy."

So Beatrice accepted the crown and everyone **CHEERED**.

THE SECRET TO BEAUTY

True beauty comes from within. A beautiful smile, confidence, and a kind heart are more important than expensive clothes or jewelry. Those who truly know how to love do not look for it on the surface — they know to find it in their hearts.

Toward the Kingdom
of the Fairies

WHO ARE YOU?

Back aboard Horizon, we sailed toward the Kingdom of the Fairies.

The air smelled fresh and clean, and a *cool wind* tickled my whiskers. I closed my eyes and sighed. Now all I needed was a **CHEESY SANDWICH**....

I was still dreaming about sandwiches when a voice said, "Sir Knight, are you **ASLEEP**?" I

opened my eyes and looked around, but there was no one in sight.

"Oh, good, you're awake," continued the voice. "I just wanted to point out the beautiful sunset."

I whirled around. There was no one in sight. My heart started **POUNDING**. Was I still dreaming? Had my cheese finally slipped off its cracker?

"Wh-wh-who are you?" I squeaked.

Then I heard someone giggling. "Oh, Knight, did you forget?" asked the voice. "It's me, Horizon."

I turned **RED** from my snout to my tail. How embarrassing! How humiliating! How could I forget we were sailing on a talking ship?!

I tried to pretend I hadn't forgotten, but Horizon was onto me. She **teased** me for the rest of the trip.

Finally, one morning, Gray began jumping up and down. At first I thought he had **FLEAS**, but then I saw it. The Kingdom of the Gnomes appeared in the distance.

I could also make out dots of color — flowers! The snow had melted.

SPRING had returned.

That night we all talked **excitedly** about our adventures.

I noticed that Blossom and GRIM chatted together.

Maybe they were discussing the future of their kingdoms. . . .

I MUST TELL YOU SOMETHING!

The next morning, we reached the coast of the Kingdom of the Gnomes. Then we took the trail up the river to the lawn of the **Great Assembly**.

When we got off the ship, a happy crowd gathered around us.

BOILS greeted me. "*Sir Knight*, I must tell you something!" he whispered.

But before he could tell me, the gnomes **LIFTED** me into the air.

They carried me proudly through the streets.

A moment later I felt something pull at my *tail*.

Then I heard Boils's voice a SECOND time.

"I must tell you something!" he said.

I was about to answer him when the *Queen of the Fairies* clapped her hands together.

"I have an **announcement**," she declared.

"Let us all assemble on the Great Lawn."

At that moment everyone began *whispering*.

"What's going on?" "Is the queen taking a **vacation**?" "Is she joining a ROCK BAND?"

In the middle of all those voices, I could also hear **Boils** trying to get my attention.

But then everyone began shouting:

"Long Live the Fantasy Company! Hooray for Our Heroes!"

HOORAY FOR EVERYONE!

When we had gathered, Blossom and Grim stood, holding hands and smiling at each other. Their shimmering BLUE LIGHT shone over the crowd.

"We have some great news," Blossom said.

"We have fallen in *love* and have decided to get *married*," Grim announced. "The Land of Nightmares will once again be called the Kingdom of Dreams."

"HOORAY FOR BLOSSOM! HOORAY FOR GRIM!" the crowd cheered.

"Oh, and, um, I'm changing my name to **George**," Grim added.

Good idea, I thought. I mean, who would want a name like **GRIM**? It reminded me of one of my coworkers at *The Rodent's Gazette*, **SYLVESTER ANTHONY DIZZY**. His initials spelled the word **SAD**. How depressing!

Strongheart interrupted my thoughts. "We're going to *tie the knot*, too!" he announced, putting his arm around Beatrice.

"HOORAY FOR THE GIANTS!" the crowd cheered.

Suddenly, I noticed something **green** jumping up and down. It was Boils.

"Me, too! Me, too!" he shouted. "I'm getting married, too! And someday we want to have lots of little chameleon babies!"

"HOORAY FOR THE CHAMELEONS!" the crowd cheered.

"Congratulations, Boils!" I told my friend. "But where is your **BRIDE-TO-BE**?"

Boils pointed to a bush. "Right here," he said.

But I couldn't see her. She had **CAMOUFLAGED** herself! So I said, "Congratulations!" to the bush, and it replied, "Thank you!"

Then I asked Boils to tell me how the two of them had met. **Big mistake!** Boils chatted for **hours**!

He told me about their first date, the movie they saw, and how much **rainbow-colored** candy they ate. Cheese niblets, that chameleon can talk!

Before everyone left, Blossom made one more announcement. "In seven days there will be a party at the Crystal Castle. We will have a *triple wedding*, and everyone in the Kingdom of Fantasy is invited!"

I clapped along with the crowd. Everyone was excited about the **big event**. Then I felt a **tug** on my sleeve. It was Beatrice. She stood chewing on her fingernails and running her fingers through her hair.

"Sir Knight," she whispered. "Can you help me? I can't get married looking like this. I look terrible!"

I thought for a minute. Then I grinned. I knew exactly who could help Beatrice: the Queen of the Gnomes!

NOT BAD AT ALL!

I was right. Queen Cozy knew exactly what to do. She took one look at Beatrice's **RIPPED** dress and **soot-covered** face and shook her head.

"Oh yes, oh yes, you do need a *makeover*, my dear," she said. "But don't worry. I'll have you looking like a movie **STAR** in no time!"

Then she climbed up a **LONNNNNG** ladder and examined Beatrice's skin with a magnifying glass.

"Hmmm . . . not bad," she said. "Not bad at all. All you need is a warm, relaxing bubble bath, a CUCUMBER facial mask, a protein-enriched shampoo-and-conditioning treatment, a *trim* to get rid of any split ends, a **manicure**, some makeup, and a *wedding gown*, and you'll be **good to go**!"

Beatrice looked like she was going to **FAINT**. But Queen Cozy just patted her hand and said, "Don't worry, deary. It will all be over before you know it. And I promise, you'll feel like a **BRAND-NEW WOMAN**. You'll be the most *beautiful* bride ever!"

At that moment a team of gnomes arrived. They rolled up their sleeves and yelled all together, "ONE BRAND-NEW WOMAN COMING UP!"

FEELING BEAUTIFUL!

Practicing good hygiene helps us feel beautiful inside and out. Brushing your teeth, taking a bath, and combing your hair are all ways to make yourself feel special. You don't need to go to an expensive spa — just fill up the tub with your favorite bubble bath!

They set to work at once, racing around like **BEES** in a hive. First they scrubbed her clean. Then they trimmed her hair. Then they applied a little lip color and made her a BEAUTIFUL WHITE wedding gown and a DeLiCAte veil.

BEATRICE'S BOUQUET

Orange blossoms for the bride

BRIDE'S SPECIAL TREATMENT

First a nice scented bubble bath with lots of bubbles . . .

A cucumber beauty mask . . .

A special herbal shampoo . . .

A special manicure for the bride with light pink nail polish . . .

A hair trim . . .

Some curlers . . .

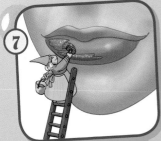

A touch of pink lipstick . . .

A beautiful gown . . .

A veil with a crown . . .

And to top it off, a spritz of perfume!

NOT ANOTHER POEM!

The following week, three couples walked down the CRYSTAL paths of the Kingdom of the Fairies.

The fairies sprinkled *rose petals*, filling the meadow with their *sweet* scent. Beatrice **beamed** in her new white wedding gown made with love by the gnomes. Boils chatted away to his *blushing* bride-to-be the whole way down the aisle. And Blossom and George *glowed* a fabumouse shade of **blue**.

The couples exchanged wedding bands.

Then Gray shouted, "Now that we're done with the mushy stuff, let's PARTAAAAY!"

Strings, the blue violin from the TALKING FOREST, began to play. First the brides and grooms danced a special dance with each other. Then the rest of the guests joined in.

Everyone was having a great time, **laughing** and dancing, when suddenly

Strings, the talking violin

Scribblehopper began hopping **UP** and **DOWN**.

"Attention!" he croaked, waving his feathered pen. "I have written a poem for this happy occasion."

Everyone groaned.

"No! No!" they cried. "NOT ANOTHER POEM!"

Scribblehopper's face fell. I felt sorry for him. I mean, even though the frog knew that everyone thought his poems were awful, he still liked to read them.

I pulled Scribblehopper aside and told him I'd listen to his poem. It was so **long** I almost fell asleep halfway through it!

 The party continued until the sun set on the CRYSTAL CASTLE.

When a shooting STAR crossed in the night, Scribblehopper and I each made a wish.

I wished that it would always be springtime all year long, and that peace would reign in the hearts of people around the WORLD!

THE SMELL OF PIZZA!

At midnight, Beatrice appeared in the doorway of the fairies' kitchen. "I hope everyone is hungry," she said. "I've prepared a typical dish from the **KINGDOM OF THE SOUTHERN GIANTS**."

I sniffed the air. It smelled like tomatoes, garlic, basil, and **cheese**. Immediately, my mouth began to water: It was **PIZZA**!

I gobbled down five **HUMONGOUS** slices in record time.

"Take a breath!" Scribblehopper teased. But I couldn't stop myself. Beatrice's pizza was **out of this world**!

I wondered how I could order it back home in New Mouse City.

KNIGHT OF THE SILVER ROSE

As soon as I thought about New Mouse City, I began to feel **homesick**. A tear came to my eye. I thought about *The Rodent's Gazette* and my friends at work. Then I thought about my family: my **daredevil** sister, Thea, my *dear* nephew Benjamin, my **STINGY** grandfather William Shortpaws, and my annoying cousin Trap. Yes, I missed them all.

So I made an announcement: "Friends, I am **sad** to leave you, but it is time I return to my world. I must go home."

EXPRESS YOUR FEELINGS!

Don't be afraid to say how you feel. If you are feeling sad, or scared, or lonely, share your feelings with a friend or a family member. You will feel a lot better if you open up to others.

I changed out of the suit of armor I had received from Horizon, the talking ship, and put on my old clothes. I have to admit, it would have been fun to return to New Mouse City wearing **armor**. Would my friends think I had become a *royal knight*? Would they think I was testing out a Halloween costume? Or would they just think I had lost my marbles?

I guess I would never know.

I said good-bye to Blossom and George. The queen gave me a sparkling rose. "I name you the Knight of the Silver Rose," she said. "Thank you, Sir Geronimo, for your bravery."

The queen pinned the silver rose on my jacket.

Then she insisted that I ride the **Unicorn of Dreams** home. The Unicorn of Dreams is a beautiful **WHITE** unicorn with wings as soft as **FEATHERS**. I was a little afraid to sit on the back of a unicorn. What if I slipped and fell and broke every bone in my body? But I didn't want to insult the queen, so I said, *"I'd be honored!"*

I said good-bye to my friends in the Kingdom of Fantasy. Then I climbed aboard the unicorn and off we flew. The clouds *zipped* by under the unicorn's hooves and I hung on tight. Even though I tried

The Order of the Silver Rose

The Knights of the Silver Rose are the defenders of the Queen of the Fairies. They must defend goodness always.

not to look, I knew that the Kingdom of Fairies was growing **smaller** and **smaller** beneath us.

After a little while, it felt like we had flown right into the center of a tornado. My whiskers trembled with fright.

...AROUND and **AROUND** we spun, faster and faster and faster and faster and faster and faster and faster and faster!......

I tried to grab on to the unicorn's neck so I wouldn't fall, but I slipped off. *"HEEEEEEELLLLLLLP!"*

The Return to
Mouse Island

A Cheesy
Good Day!

I woke up with a start. What had happened?

I found myself in the bathroom of my house. **Ouch**, what a headache!

Suddenly, I remembered. I had gone to the bathroom looking for a BANDAGE. Then I had slipped in a puddle of water, because the toilet was **dripping** and I hadn't called the plumber. I must have hit my head on the sink.

What a bUmp!!!

I massaged my head as I peered out the window. It was already morning. I thought about the dream I'd had that night. It had been all about traveling through the Kingdom of Fantasy.

I smiled. Every time I went there, I had the most **AMAZING** adventures!

I got up and called the plumber. Then I made myself a delicious **cheesy** morning milk shake. **YUM!**

Later on, I left the house to go for a walk. As I walked, I whistled a **happy** tune. I was so

glad to be home in New Mouse City. The air was FRESH and CLEAN and filled with the scent of flowers. Oh, how I love springtime!

Life is good, the world is wonderful, and everything's coming up roses!

OH, HOW I ADORE THAT MOUSE!

I headed to the New Mouse City Park. Have you ever been there? It is one of the most *beautiful* parks on all of Mouse Island.

The park was filled with mice enjoying the **beautiful** weather. I saw families with picnic baskets and young mouselets on *swings*. I saw chili cheese dog vendors pushing their carts. Overhead the *peach* trees were in full bloom, and nests held all kinds of *chirping* birds.

I was looking up at the trees when I ran right into someone. **OOPS!** How embarrassing! I looked up. The mouse I'd run into started to *giggle*. Now I was even more embarrassed. It was my friend **Petunia Pretty Paws**!

I have had a crush on Petunia for the longest time, but I never seem to be able to get up the **courage** to tell her.

Just then I spied a *four-leaf* clover in the grass. I gave it to Petunia.

"Here, Petunia," I said. "This four-leaf clover is for you. I hope it brings lots and lots of luck."

Petunia smiled. "Oh, G, you are so sweet!" she squeaked. Then, before I knew what hit me, she gave me a little kiss on the ear.

Kiss!

I turned three shades of **red**. "Well, thanks, Neptunia — I mean, Penutia — I mean, Petunia," I mumbled.

I was so happy I tripped over my own two paws and ran away with my heart **BEATING** a million miles a minute. Oh, how I *adore* that mouse!!

RUSS T. PIPE

At that moment my cell phone rang. It was the plumber, **Russ T. Pipe**. He was on his way over to my house.

I ran home in a hurry.

"Thank you for coming so quickly," I told Mr. Pipe when he arrived. In fact, Mr. Pipe was so nice I made him a delicious PINEAPPLE cream cheese smoothie.

"So, how did you get such a BUMP on your head?" he asked me as he set to work.

I told him about slipping in the PUDDLE. Then I told him all about the Kingdom of Fantasy.

As I told the story, Mr. Pipe listened, fascinated. "And then what happened?" he kept asking. "And then what?"

Waaaaa!

At one point, he started to cry. He blew his nose in some **TOILET PAPER**. "Oh, this is such a beautiful, touching story," he sobbed. "There are even **THREE** weddings! And the giant found his SOUL Mate!"

He cried so much he ended up **flooding** my bathroom again!

"Thank you for such a heartwarming story," he said when I was finished. "It was so nice to hear, I will fix your toilet for **fRee**."

Before Mr. Pipe left my house, he gave me a great IDEA.

"You are a writer, right, Mr. Stilton?" he asked.

I didn't realize that my story was so moving. . . .

"Yes," I said.

"Well, you should write a **book** about the Kingdom of Fantasy. I mean, it's got everything in it. It's got funny parts, like the skunk **stinking up** everything and the cat leaving FISH BONES in the giant's hat. And it's got **sweet** parts, like when the chameleons find each other, even though they're kind of hard to find with all that camouflaging. And it's got **SCARY** parts, like the Smoke-spitting Volcano and Cackle and Grim's sword fight."

I shivered when I thought about Cackle. Yes, my story had **SCARY** parts. But luckily, there were lots of **happy** parts, too.

After Russ T. Pipe left, I filled the tub up and made myself a nice **HOT** bath with lots and lots of BUBBLES. Ah, how I loved my bubble baths!

What a great idea!

I scrubbed my fur until it **gleamed**, sailed my rubber ducky, and pretended I was **Santa Mouse** with a bubble beard (but that's just between you and me).

While I was relaxing, I thought about what the plumber had said. I *could* write a nice book about my return to the Kingdom of Fantasy. After all, I had already written two books about my adventures there, and they had both been big hits. So that was what I decided to do: I would write a book about my third trip to the Kingdom of Fantasy!

Here is a collection of maps
From the Kingdom of Fantasy

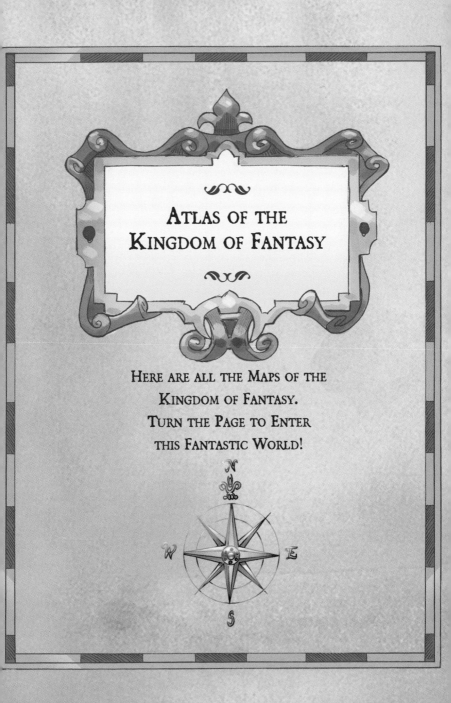

ATLAS OF THE KINGDOM OF FANTASY

HERE ARE ALL THE MAPS OF THE
KINGDOM OF FANTASY.
TURN THE PAGE TO ENTER
THIS FANTASTIC WORLD!

*The KINGDOM OF FANTASY is marvelous
and all you have to do to get there is dream!
There are many, many kingdoms: Some are dark and
scary, and others are full of light and happiness.*

There is the scary KINGDOM OF THE WITCHES,
where the wicked Cackle reigns, but there is also
the melodious KINGDOM OF THE MERMAIDS.

There is the dangerous KINGDOM OF THE FIRE
DRAGONS, but also the sweet KINGDOM OF THE
SILVER DRAGONS, where Sterling, the courageous
dragon tamer, lives.

There are the funny KINGDOM OF THE
PIXIES, where the pixies love to tell jokes, and
the green KINGDOM OF THE GNOMES, which
is home to forests and nature.

There are the freezing KINGDOM
OF THE NORTHERN GIANTS,
where Strongheart the Giant is from,
and the hot KINGDOM OF THE
SOUTHERN GIANTS, where Beatrice Bigfoot,
the last lady giant, is from.

There are the KINGDOM OF THE ELVES,
where you can find King Thunderhorn's castle,
the LAND OF THE FAIRY TALES, and the fantastic
TALKING FOREST. Finally, there is the luminous
KINGDOM OF THE FAIRIES, where Blossom, the
Queen of the KINGDOM OF FANTASY, lives.

Fantasian Alphabet

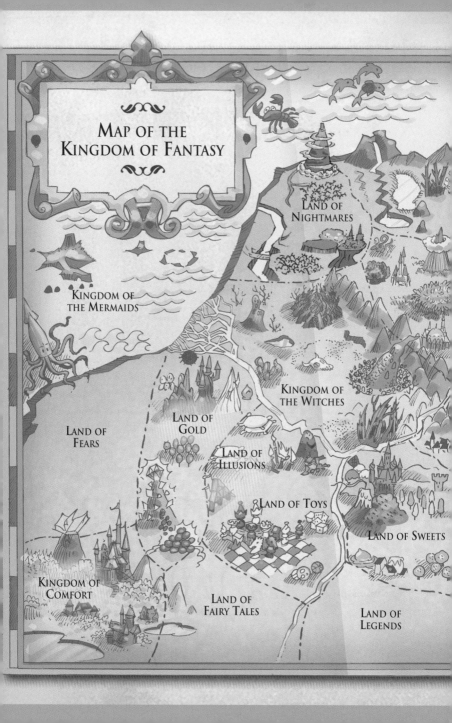

MAP OF THE
KINGDOM OF FANTASY

LAND OF
NIGHTMARES

KINGDOM OF
THE MERMAIDS

KINGDOM OF
THE WITCHES

LAND OF
FEARS

LAND OF
GOLD

LAND OF
ILLUSIONS

LAND OF TOYS

LAND OF SWEETS

KINGDOM OF
COMFORT

LAND OF
FAIRY TALES

LAND OF
LEGENDS

SEA OF
DREAMS

KINGDOM
OF THE
PIXIES

KINGDOM
OF THE FIRE
DRAGONS

KINGDOM OF
THE GNOMES

TALKING
FOREST

KINGDOM OF
THE FAIRIES

KINGDOM OF THE ELVES

LAND OF THE
OGRES

KINGDOM OF
THE NORTHERN
GIANTS

KINGDOM OF
THE SILVER
DRAGONS

LAND OF
GHOSTS

KINGDOM OF THE
SOUTHERN GIANTS

EARTH MILE   0 1 2 3 4 5
MARINE MILE   0 1 2 3 4 5
FANTASIAN MILE 0 1 2 3 4 5

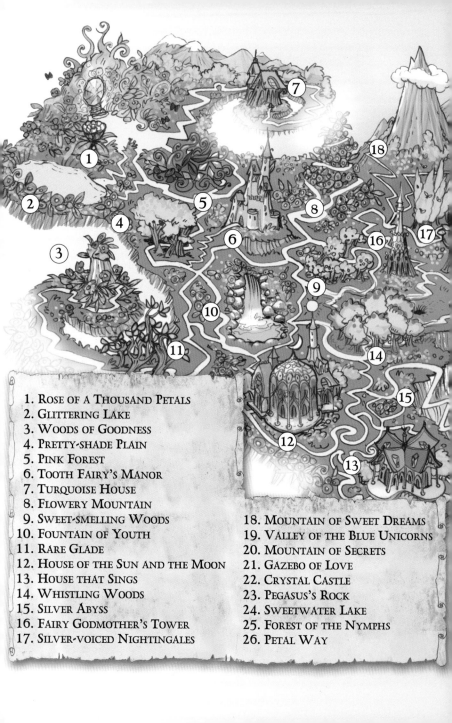

1. ROSE OF A THOUSAND PETALS
2. GLITTERING LAKE
3. WOODS OF GOODNESS
4. PRETTY-SHADE PLAIN
5. PINK FOREST
6. TOOTH FAIRY'S MANOR
7. TURQUOISE HOUSE
8. FLOWERY MOUNTAIN
9. SWEET-SMELLING WOODS
10. FOUNTAIN OF YOUTH
11. RARE GLADE
12. HOUSE OF THE SUN AND THE MOON
13. HOUSE THAT SINGS
14. WHISTLING WOODS
15. SILVER ABYSS
16. FAIRY GODMOTHER'S TOWER
17. SILVER-VOICED NIGHTINGALES
18. MOUNTAIN OF SWEET DREAMS
19. VALLEY OF THE BLUE UNICORNS
20. MOUNTAIN OF SECRETS
21. GAZEBO OF LOVE
22. CRYSTAL CASTLE
23. PEGASUS'S ROCK
24. SWEETWATER LAKE
25. FOREST OF THE NYMPHS
26. PETAL WAY

KINGDOM OF THE FAIRIES

THE LAND OF FAIRY TALES

KINGDOM OF THE SILVER DRAGONS

1. CRYSTAL CAVES
2. STERLING'S PALACE
3. SECRET PASSAGE
4. DIVING BOARD
5. DRAGON LAKE
6. SILVER RIVER
7. NURSERY
8. ROCK BRIDGE
9. HOSPITAL
10. OUTDOOR THEATER
11. GYM
12. CONTROL TOWER
13. ARENA FOR COMPETITIONS
14. LANDING AREA
15. LIBRARY

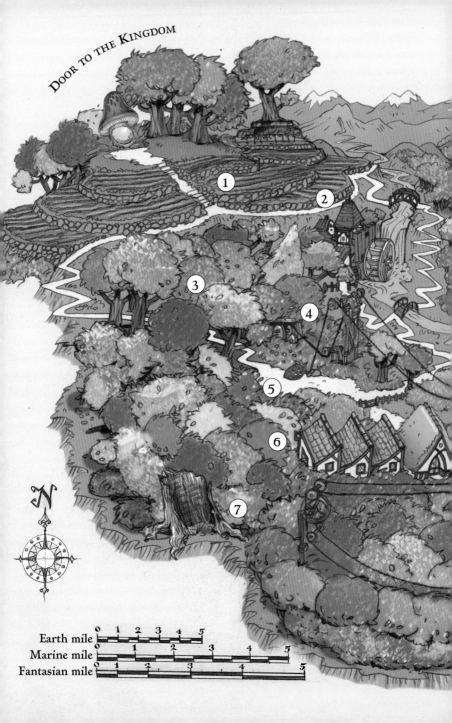

DOOR TO THE KINGDOM

N

Earth mile   0 1 2 3 4 5
Marine mile   0 1 2 3 4 5
Fantasian mile 0 1 2 3 4 5

The Kingdom of the Gnomes

LAND OF NIGHTMARES

1. THRONE OF POWER
2. PERMANENT CLOUDS
3. VOLCANO OF NIGHTMARES
4. DESERT OF FIRE AND ICE
5. INSOMNIA CLIFF
6. SPITFIRE GEYSER
7. HAUNTED LAKE
8. PRICKLY FOREST
9. WHISPERING WOODS
10. PANIC LAKE
11. SLOBBER SWAMP
12. ANXIETY PLATEAU
13. CASTLE OF OLD DREAMS
14. BRUISE LAGOON
15. RIVER OF LOST MEMORIES
16. STENCH FOREST
17. SMOKE-SPITTING VOLCANO
18. MONSTER PEAK
19. VERTIGO BRIDGE
20. CHASM OF FEAR
21. SHIVER BEACH
22. GULF OF SAD AWAKENINGS

DOOR TO THE KINGDOM

The Kingdom of the Giants

KINGDOM OF THE ELVES

1. SOLITARY ELF PEAK
2. THE WHITE CASTLE
   (CITY OF THE ELVES)
3. SPARKLING RIVER
4. FOUNTAIN OF YOUTH
5. DEER CASTLE
6. VALLEY OF THE WIND
7. WELL OF HAPPY
   THOUGHTS
8. FLOWER TOWER
9. SAGE MOUNTAIN
10. CONFIDENCE BRIDGE
11. TOP OF THE CLOUDS PEAK
12. SWEET SONG FALLS
13. SERENITY LAKE
14. EVERGREEN FOREST
15. SECRET PASSAGE
16. SILVER WOODS
17. PATH OF A THOUSAND
    YEARS

TALKING FOREST

1. ECHO PEAK
2. RUMOR FALLS
3. PORT OF TRANQUILITY
4. GREAT TALKING TREE
5. BLUE WOODS
6. MUSIC WOODS
7. CRICKET FIELD
8. OLIVE TREES FOR PEACE
9. MUSICAL NOTES FIELD

THE END

This is the end of this voyage through the

Kingdom of Fantasy. Now go live your

life day by day with commitment, courage,

love, and above all, a sense of adventure!

ABOUT THE AUTHOR

Born in New Mouse City, Mouse Island, **GERONIMO STILTON** is Rattus Emeritus of Mousomorphic Literature and of Neo-Ratonic Comparative Philosophy. For the past twenty years, he has been running *The Rodent's Gazette*, New Mouse City's most widely read daily newspaper.

Stilton was awarded the Ratitzer Prize for his scoops on *The Curse of the Cheese Pyramid* and *The Search for Sunken Treasure*. He has also received the Andersen 2000 Prize for Personality of the Year. One of his bestsellers won the 2002 eBook Award for world's best ratlings' electronic book. His works have been published all over the globe.

In his spare time, Mr. Stilton collects antique cheese rinds and plays golf. But what he most enjoys is telling stories to his nephew Benjamin.

And don't miss any of my other fabumouse adventures!

#1 Lost Treasure of the Emerald Eye

#2 The Curse of the Cheese Pyramid

#3 Cat and Mouse in a Haunted House

#4 I'm Too Fond of My Fur!

#5 Four Mice Deep in the Jungle

#6 Paws Off, Cheddarface!

#7 Red Pizzas for a Blue Count

#8 Attack of the Bandit Cats

#9 A Fabumouse Vacation for Geronimo

#10 All Because of a Cup of Coffee

#11 It's Halloween, You 'Fraidy Mouse!

#12 Merry Christmas, Geronimo!

#13 The Phantom of the Subway

#14 The Temple of the Ruby of Fire

#15 The Mona Mousa Code

#16 A Cheese-Colored Camper

#17 Watch Your Whiskers, Stilton!

#18 Shipwreck on the Pirate Islands

#19 My Name Is Stilton, Geronimo Stilton

#20 Surf's Up, Geronimo!

#21 The Wild, Wild West

#22 The Secret of Cacklefur Castle

A Christmas Tale

#23 Valentine's Day Disaster

#24 Field Trip to Niagara Falls

#25 The Search for Sunken Treasure

#26 The Mummy with No Name

#27 The Christmas Toy Factory

#28 Wedding Crasher

#29 Down and Out Down Under

#30 The Mouse Island Marathon

#31 The Mysterious Cheese Thief

Christmas Catastrophe

#32 Valley of the Giant Skeletons

#33 Geronimo and the Gold Medal Mystery

#34 Geronimo Stilton, Secret Agent

#35 A Very Merry Christmas

#36 Geronimo's Valentine

#37 The Race Across America

#38 A Fabumouse School Adventure

#39 Singing Sensation

#40 The Karate Mouse

#41 Mighty Mount Kilimanjaro

#42 The Peculiar Pumpkin Thief

#43 I'm Not a Supermouse!

#44 The Giant Diamond Robbery

#45 Save the White Whale!

#46 The Haunted Castle

And coming soon!

#47 Run for the Hills, Geronimo!

If you like my brother Geronimo's books, check out these exciting adventures of the Thea Sisters!

Meet
CREEPELLA VON CACKLEFUR

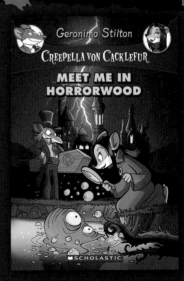

I, *Geronimo Stilton*, have a lot of mouse friends, but none as **spooky** as my friend CREEPELLA VON CACKLEFUR! She is an enchanting and MYSTERIOUS mouse with a pet bat named Bitewing. YIKES! I'm a real 'fraidy mouse, but even I think CREEPELLA and her family are AWFULLY fascinating. I can't wait for you to read all about CREEPELLA in these fa-mouse-ly funny and **spectacularly spooky** tales!

#1 THE THIRTEEN GHOSTS

#2 MEET ME IN HORRORWOOD

And don't miss my first two journeys through the Kingdom of Fantasy!

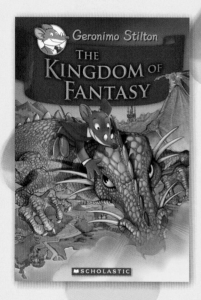

THE KINGDOM OF FANTASY

THE QUEST FOR PARADISE:
THE RETURN TO THE KINGDOM OF FANTASY